Don't think. Act...

Jason's skin was hot to the touch, and damn if he didn't smell good.

He arched one eyebrow at Molly but didn't make another move. She felt the unspoken dare between them. Was she going to do this or back away as she had earlier?

"Hell."

His curse lingered in the air around them as his mouth came down on hers. For a mouth that had always looked so strong and tough, it was soft against hers. He took the kiss slowly as if he had all the time in the world.

They had this night.

He tasted of whiskey and temptation. Two things she knew she should resist right now but was unable to.

She was tired of denying herself Jason McCoy.

She'd wanted him for longer than she could remember...and at last it seemed he was hers for the taking.

Dear Reader,

Hello! Welcome to the first book in my new series, Space Cowboys. I was born just before man walked on the moon, and my mom has an 8mm film of me crawling on the floor while in the background the television is tuned to that historic moon landing. From a very early age I wanted to be an astronaut—it seemed fun. Unfortunately for me you have to be really good at science and advanced math... something I'm not.

However, I am good at reading and researching, and when a conversation with my editor about how ranching is a major industry in parts of Florida (including the part where I grew up) turned to a "what if," Space Cowboys was born. I got to combine two things that I love a lot, space—and the vast universe—and ranching. The series is set in Texas instead of Florida because all training at NASA takes place in Texas.

I had a lot of fun writing this book. I lived in Texas for five wonderful years and revisiting Texas through this story was like going home. I also love Jason and Molly, both strong-willed people who never take the easy path. They always stand by what they think is right, even if that means letting go of each other.

I hope you enjoy the first book in the Space Cowboys series!

Happy reading,

Katherine

Katherine Garbera

—

No Limits

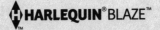

Recycling programs
for this product may
not exist in your area.

ISBN-13: 978-0-373-79914-5

No Limits

Copyright © 2016 by Katherine Garbera

This edition published by arrangement with Harlequin Books S.A.

For questions and comments about the quality of this book, please contact us at CustomerService@Harlequin.com.

® and TM are trademarks of Harlequin Enterprises Limited or its corporate affiliates. Trademarks indicated with ® are registered in the United States Patent and Trademark Office, the Canadian Intellectual Property Office and in other countries.

Printed in U.S.A.

USA TODAY bestselling author **Katherine Garbera** is a two-time MAGGIE® Award winner who has written more than seventy books. A Florida native who grew up to travel the globe, Katherine now makes her home in the Midlands of the UK with her husband, two children and a very spoiled miniature dachshund. Visit Katherine on the web at katherinegarbera.com, or catch up with her on Facebook and Twitter.

Books by Katherine Garbera

Harlequin Blaze

One More Kiss
Sizzle

Holiday Heat

In Too Close
Under the Mistletoe
After Midnight

Harlequin Desire

Miami Nights

Taming the VIP Playboy
Seducing His Opposition
Reunited...With Child

Baby Business

His Instant Heir
Bound by a Child
For Her Son's Sake

To get the inside scoop on Harlequin Blaze and its talented writers, be sure to check out blazeauthors.com.

All backlist available in ebook format.

Visit the Author Profile page at Harlequin.com for more titles.

This book is dedicated to my darling husband, Rob Elser. Thanks for sharing your love of science and the universe with me and helping to sow the seeds of this series.

Acknowledgments
Thanks to my editor Laura Barth for helping to turn an offhand comment about astronauts and the Florida ranching community into a viable series idea.

1

THE DOOR OPENED. Ace McCoy couldn't see the figure standing on the porch due to distance and the shadow cast by the setting sun, but his gut told him it was *her*. And if he was a betting man, he'd wager she was more beautiful than she'd been at sixteen when he'd walked away without a backward glance.

He walked slowly toward the house; her dad had once said that the only way to move forward was past fear. And, though he wasn't truly afraid of Molly Tanner, she was the one woman who had haunted him all of his life. Seeing her again after thirteen years made his gut clench.

"Jason—I mean 'Ace'—McCoy," she said, as if his call sign left a bad taste in her mouth. "Thought you'd never set foot on this ranch again."

He was right. She'd matured into her features. The mouth that had once seemed too big was now full and sensuous. Her eyes were still as rich as dark chocolate and her brows were thick and serious. Her nose was pert and some would say cute. But he'd been on the receiving end of her temper, so cute wasn't a word he'd use to describe her.

Her breasts were fuller than he remembered, her waist smaller, more nipped in. And her hips—*ah, hell*—those hips were curvy, beckoning a man to squeeze them and pull her closer. He still remembered the feel of her in his arms, the taste of her mouth, even though they'd only shared one forbidden kiss.

"I'm back because of your dad," he said, taking off his cowboy hat as he stepped up onto the wooden porch that extended across the front of the house. There were two large clay pots on either side of the stairs and four wooden rocking chairs beckoned. But he knew better than to drop his guard. Not yet.

Maybe not ever.

In Houston he felt like a man in control, a man in charge of his destiny and his life. But a problem with the recovery of his bone density, revealed in his last post-flight medical exam, had him grounded indefinitely. And his mentor—the closest thing he had to a father—had left him half of this ranch. Returning to Cole's Hill, Texas, made him feel as if he was stepping into the past, a past he preferred to leave behind.

The boy he'd been. The trouble that had dogged him. The stolen kiss that had cost him this, the only home he'd ever really had.

"He's dead."

"I know. I…"

"Don't make excuses," she said. "He always hoped you'd come back, and I guess he found the one way to get you here."

"Dying is extreme even for him."

"Yeah, it was," she said, tears sparkling in her eyes

as she turned away and dropped her chin to her chest. "It was so unexpected."

He reached out and put his hand on her shoulder, needing to offer comfort and maybe find some himself. Mick had been a young sixty-five, and Ace was still shocked that an all-terrain-vehicle accident had claimed his mentor's life.

Molly wiped her eyes with her hand and then stepped back from him. Her voice broke as she started to speak, so she cleared her throat and tried again. "He named you in his will."

"I was surprised. He and I made our peace," he said. "But the terms of his will caught me off guard."

"Me, too," she said. "I'm still processing the fact that he's gone."

"I would have come back for the funeral, but I was on the space station." He was a commander with NASA who had dreams of being one of the first astronauts to set out on the long-term missions necessary to prepare for space travel to Mars. Upon returning from space this time, he'd undergone intensive rehabilitation in Houston to regain the strength and muscle astronauts lose from spending so much time in microgravity. For a while, he'd had trouble walking and couldn't drive, so his trip to the ranch had been postponed until now.

"I know," she said. "Dad was proud of you...of what you accomplished. Come on in."

"You sure about that?" he asked.

At the moment he'd rather be pulling Gs during a launch, fighting the urge to throw up, than standing here. He'd always been more comfortable observing Earth than being on it. Nothing new there.

"Yes. It's your place, too," she said. She turned on her heel, disappearing into the house, leaving a trail of strawberry-scented air in her wake and more than a little regret. To be fair, the regret could be coming from him.

He stood there for a long minute, looking at the wooden frame, remembering the boy he'd been at fourteen when he'd first arrived at the ranch. He'd been surly, stand-offish, with a black eye and a busted lip. Molly had greeted him that day, too. She'd stood there with her long chestnut braids, watching him. He'd made some smart-ass comment and she'd put him in his place and walked away.

From that moment on he'd been following her. Even leaving the ranch, going into the military and becoming an astronaut had been about following her. The only man who could catch Molly was one who was aiming for the stars. He wanted to prove that he was more than the juvenile delinquent she'd met all those years ago. The boy-man who wasn't good enough to kiss her or touch her.

"You coming or not, space cowboy?"

He shook off the mantle of the past, opening the screen door to follow her. It snapped shut behind him and his boots echoed as he walked down the hall to the kitchen. He paused when he noticed a framed photo on the wall. He put his hand next to it, staring at the image of himself in uniform with Mick standing so proudly next to him.

Yeah, the regret was all his.

He should have come back sooner, years ago when Mick had asked. But he'd been afraid of running into Molly. Afraid he'd ask more from her than a kiss. He'd known once he went down that road with her there'd be no coming back. And even as a teen he'd realized there was no real future for him on the ranch.

NASA hadn't just given him a career; they'd given him a life he was proud of, a life he loved, and he didn't want to risk being tied to the ground by emotions or expectations.

Ace wasn't too sure who he was if he wasn't in space. He felt that uncertainty more than ever now, with three months' leave stretching in front of him. His commander wanted him to take a break before his follow-up medical exam and he was due for some time off, anyway. He was on a strict exercise regimen to regain bone density. Being outside the Earth's gravitational field had an adverse effect on the human body and the doctors were monitoring Ace's recovery closely to ensure astronauts sent on long-term missions wouldn't suffer lasting damage.

"Jason?" she asked.

It felt strange to hear her say his name. He didn't know who Jason was anymore. That mixed-up delinquent from the time before he'd joined the military and NASA? The boy whose mother had left him to fend for himself? "Call me Ace."

She rolled her eyes. "I'll try, but you've always been Jason to me," she said. "I don't remember you being this slow, though."

"Maybe you don't know everything about me."

"Oh, that's one thing I'm sure of."

"You pissed at me for something?" he asked as he followed her down the hall and into the brightly lit kitchen.

"What would I have to be pissed about?" she asked. "We haven't seen each other since I was sixteen."

"Maybe that's it exactly."

She didn't say a word, just stretched to open the cabinet over the sink. The hem of her blouse hitched up revealing the small of her back and her raspberry birthmark. She cursed and braced her hand on the countertop as she reached for the bottle of Maker's Mark that was just out of reach.

Ace came up behind her, putting his hand on the small of her back. Unable to resist, he rubbed his finger over the birthmark as he reached over her head and snagged the bottle.

She made a startled noise and turned.

He stared down into those big chocolate-brown eyes and knew that all the years and all the distance he'd put between them didn't matter. He still wanted her just as fiercely as he always had. He put the bottle on the counter behind her.

Her eyelids dropped halfway and a strand of hair fell across her face. He gently brushed it back behind her ear. With one hand on the small of her back and the other on her face, he leaned down and felt the exhalation of her minty breath against his lips.

Their lips touched for the barest of seconds, and then her eyes flew open.

"Well, howdy! I thought you weren't ever coming back this way, Ace."

He stepped back, keeping one hand on Molly, and turned to greet Rina Holmes, the housekeeper of the Bar T Ranch.

"Sorry for interrupting. I didn't realize you'd already started the homecoming," Rina said.

"There is no homecoming going on here, Rina. Jas—Ace helped me reach Dad's whiskey. We are going to have a toast to him. You're just in time to join us," Molly said, tugging down the hem of her blouse as she moved away from him.

"Looked like a helluva lot more than that to me," Rina said.

The housekeeper was in her fifties but looked more like forty. She wore her reddish-blond hair hanging around her shoulders. She had an easy smile and a curvy figure, and she'd been on the ranch since before Molly was born. She pulled Jason into a big bear hug.

"We've missed you, Ace."

"I'm sorry I couldn't get here sooner," he said. He watched Molly over Rina's shoulder and noticed her hands tremble the tiniest bit as she poured three glasses of whiskey.

"Mick and me knew you were NASA's shining star. Boy, you sure surprised us," Rina said. "Never expected the punky juvenile to turn into an American hero."

"Dad did," Molly said. "Dad always believed *Ace* was going to do big things."

"He did," Rina agreed, turning and picking up one of the glasses.

"To Mick," Rina said, raising her glass.

"To Mick," Ace added.

"To Dad," Molly said and she took a deep swallow of the whiskey. He couldn't take his eyes off her mouth. He wanted to finish the kiss they'd barely started. Wanted that and a lot more. And he'd always gone after what he wanted.

He noticed that Molly still watched him with an in-

tense stare whenever Rina wasn't looking, but as they
drank more whiskey and shared stories about Mick,
the tension eased a little. And for a moment he had a
glimpse of a different future. One that wasn't written
in the stars but was tied to the land. And that made
him uncomfortable. Because it seemed more real than
it ever had before.

MOLLY COULDN'T SLEEP. She knew where the blame lay.
Just down the hall in the bedroom he'd occupied as a
teen. During dinner with the ranch foreman, Jeb, and
the hands, Jason had looked uncomfortable. He'd sat
there answering their questions about what it was like
to be an astronaut, but when everyone had headed to
the bunkhouse he'd seemed lost.

Jason "Ace" McCoy.

It would have been nice if he'd gotten soft in the
years since she'd last seen him. Maybe lost some of his
thick dark hair or developed a potbelly. But she knew
that was a foolish wish. NASA didn't choose men who
let themselves go to be part of exclusive missions. She
had kept tabs on him, even if she hadn't read every
article about the hotshot Jason had become, the way
her father always had.

She wondered sometimes if her dad had known
about her crush on Jason. Probably. She hadn't exactly
been subtle that last summer he'd been at the Bar T.

She'd been too young to really understand the raw
sexuality that was so much a part of his nature when
she'd been sixteen, but at twenty-nine—now she understood it so much better. The only thing standing
between them long ago had been his fear that her fa-

ther wouldn't approve. And she'd been too unsure of herself to be clear with Jason about what she wanted.

She slipped out of bed and pulled on her dad's flannel robe. It still smelled of his aftershave and it was the closest thing she had to getting a hug from him. She wrapped her arms around herself for a long minute before she tied the sash as she opened the door.

The old hinges creaked as she did so. The ranch needed an infusion of cash. Everything was old and tired.

Including her?

Damn.

She really hoped not, but tonight, with Jason being back and Dad being gone, she was feeling…too much. A little down, a little wild, a little angry.

The night was warm and the full moon lit her path. The upstairs bedrooms ran along a corridor that was lined with floor-to-ceiling glass panes affording a view of the acres and acres of pasture that her ancestors had claimed and kept as their own. Each generation added their own stamp to their home, which had started as a big farm house, but had evolved into something unique with modern touches. She stood there for a moment, just looking at the land. She loved Texas. And this land was in her blood. She knew she'd do whatever she had to to keep the ranch, even if it meant swallowing her pride and getting along with Jason.

She wanted to confront him. Had since the moment he'd arrived. She'd sent him a card for his birthday every year for the first five years after he left, but she'd never heard anything back. She was more than a little angry. And it was the safest emotion for her to land on at the moment.

She had a gaping sense of loss from her father's death and she knew some of the anger coursing through her was because she hadn't spent enough quality time with him before he died. Sure, they'd done chores together and eaten with Jeb and the other ranch hands and sat in silence, but she'd never really gotten to know him. She had thought she'd have decades left to hear his stories and ask him questions.

Jason's door was closed.

She reminded herself that he was no longer the boy she'd known so well...yet not well enough.

The too-brief kiss they'd shared in the kitchen had whetted her appetite, reawakened a desire that had never really gone away. He would leave again. To be fair, she'd probably want him to go. She knew she didn't share power easily and the thought of having to make decisions about the ranch with him chafed.

"Molly?"

She glanced up and saw him standing in front of his bedroom. No shirt to cover that muscled chest of his, only a pair of low-slung jeans that clung to his hip bones. His hair was rumpled as if he'd run his fingers through it a few times. Hers tingled as she thought of touching him.

"I am pissed at you," she said at last.

He rubbed his chest, the thin layer of hair there and the scar he'd earned trying to climb out his window when he'd first come to live with them. The Bar T Ranch had left its mark on Jason as surely as it had on her.

"I left so I wouldn't hurt your relationship with your dad," he said.

"That's BS and you know it. You left because you were afraid."

"Afraid?"

"Yes. *Of me*. Of getting tied to this ranch and never seeing the world outside its borders."

He shrugged and took a step forward. She shivered. He was all masculine grace. He moved as if he owned the world, and given that he'd seen it from orbit maybe he did.

She wanted to be in control. But she couldn't help wondering if giving in to lust would finally answer the question that had niggled at her for thirteen long years. Would he be the lover she'd always dreamed of? Sixteen-year-old Molly had been sure of it. Twenty-nine-year-old Molly had been disappointed by men before. But she wanted this, wanted him.

Always had.

"So..."

"You certainly aren't any more eloquent than you used to be," she said, closing the gap between them. Acting without thinking.

That was the key. *Don't think*. She had been thinking way too much since her father died and she'd seen Jason's name on the will. She'd been questioning why her father, whom she'd thought she'd known so well, had named him in the will and not just her. Did he think she needed a man's help?

Stop.

Don't think.

Act.

She put her hands on Jason's shoulders. His skin was hot, hard under her touch, and damn he smelled good. She went up on her tiptoes, hung there balanced only by her hands on his body.

He arched one eyebrow at her but didn't make another move. She felt the unspoken dare between them. Was she going to do this or back away as she had in the kitchen?

"Ah, hell."

Jason's words lingered in the air around them as his mouth came down on hers. For a mouth that had always looked so strong and tough, it was soft against hers. He took the kiss slowly as if he had all the time in the world.

They had this night.

Nothing was complicated in this empty house with the moon shining down on them. She held tightly on to his shoulders as he parted his lips and she felt the first thrust of his tongue in her mouth.

He tasted of whiskey and temptation. Two things she knew she should resist right now but was unable to.

She was tired of denying herself. Jason McCoy. She'd wanted him for longer than she could remember and at last it seemed he was hers for the taking.

No more regrets.

He settled his hands on her hips, drawing her closer, and the silk nightie she wore under the robe did nothing to protect her from the intense heat of his embrace. He thrust his tongue deeper into her mouth and she felt a fire start in her soul and fan outward.

She pulled back, looking up into his eyes. They were heavy-lidded, half-closed. Slowly he opened them.

2

MOLLY STARED UP into eyes the color of the morning sky, trying not to lose herself. She knew why she was out here in the hallway after midnight. But it was too much to believe that he'd wandered into the hall at the same moment, also unable to sleep.

"Why are you actually here?" she asked. Her voice sounded husky, needy. Too feminine. She might want to pretend Jason didn't affect her, but that would be a lie. Her father hadn't held with lying so neither would she.

"To see the land, to figure things out with you," he said, but he'd turned away. He put his hands on his hips and looked out the big window at the inky-black sky beyond. She wondered if, when he looked at the night sky, it made him long to be back among the stars.

She had questions about that part of his life, but mostly, right now, she needed to not turn something meaningless into a big deal. Her dad had died. She felt tears burning her eyes. She hoped one day she'd be able to think about him without this gut-wrenching pain, but she wasn't there yet. Would she ever be?

"Hey, you all right?"

She shook her head. "Just—"

Her voice, heavy with tears, sounded deep and almost unintelligible.

"It's okay. I miss Mick, too," he said.

Miss him. She ached with his loss. She still wasn't ready to be on her own with the ranch or in life. She needed her father's advice. Now more than ever.

More tears fell and all of a sudden she was sobbing. She had heard it said that grief was the photo negative of love, but she wasn't ready to accept it. It was just a huge hole in her that could never be filled.

Jason cursed and then pulled her into his arms. He didn't do anything else. Just held her as sobs racked her body and her emotions fell in a gush of tears. She had no idea how much time had passed until she was hiccupping softly and the tears had almost dried up.

"Sorry for that," she said, taking a step backward.

"I'm not," he admitted. He wiped the trail of moisture off her face and then sighed. "I'm also here because...I have a few health concerns after spending a year on the International Space Station and my commander wants me to take a break."

"Oh. I appreciate your honesty. So what's wrong with your health?"

"Nothing that some time in Earth's gravity shouldn't fix. Everyone is betting on that. But I'm mainly at the ranch for the reasons I gave you before—because we need to talk, to figure out what we are going to do with this place," he said.

"And kissing me was...what was that?" she asked. Oh, God, had she once again thrown herself at Jason?

What was it about him that made her abandon common sense?

Aside from his rock-hard body, chiseled jaw and brilliant blue eyes. Those were things any woman would find appealing. But she didn't normally throw herself at men just because they were attractive.

"That was us. I guess it's always been there between us, but we never really took the time to pursue it," he said.

She arched one eyebrow at him. She felt energy and anger coursing through her, but she knew focusing on these feelings was just an easy way to pretend she wasn't still missing her dad. "Pursue it?"

He shrugged. One of those gestures men make when they know better than to answer a woman.

"You just admitted you are leaving as soon as you get the all clear from NASA," she said. "We aren't pursuing anything."

"Maybe, maybe not," he said, moving closer to her. She felt the heat of his body and found it very hard to look away from his naked chest. Besides the scar on his left side, he had a tattoo that read *To boldly go*.

He took another step closer and she put her hand up. Kissing him had been foolish. She was a practical woman. She always had been. And now, with Dad gone, she really needed to think rationally. The ranch was in financial trouble, as it had been for years, and she needed to focus on that.

Not wonder what it would feel like to run her finger over Jason's tattoo.

"What are you thinking?" he asked. His voice was low and it brushed over her senses like a warm breeze. She wanted to close her eyes and tip her face up, but she didn't. She'd had her kiss. And it was hotter than she had ever expected. But now she had to go back to being Molly.

"Nothing."

Nothing. Really? She was intelligent and her remarks had been known to leave men speechless, but with Jason she felt like she was sixteen-year-old Molly in the throes of her crush.

"Well, nothing I want to talk about with you," she admitted. "I'm not myself tonight. And I want to be like Scarlett and put my troubles off for another day."

"I'm not myself, either," he admitted. "Who is Scarlett?"

"Scarlett O'Hara from *Gone with the Wind.* She's famous for saying 'Tomorrow is another day.'"

"Well, she's right," he said. "But for tonight we have two choices."

"Only two?"

"Well, two that won't get us into trouble," he said.

There was a touch of mischief in his expression and she realized it had been too long since anyone had teased her. Everyone had been treating her as if she was fragile since her dad had died.

"I'm listening."

"We can get that bottle of Maker's Mark out of the cabinet and drink until it's empty," he said.

"Or?"

"Or we can saddle up the horses and chase the moon as it moves across the sky," he said. "I recall that used to be one of your favorite things to do."

She swallowed hard. It still was.

How could a man she hadn't seen in thirteen years be the one person who knew her that well?

"Ride," she said.

"Good choice. Meet you at the stables in ten?"

She nodded and walked away from him. She didn't think as she changed into her favorite pair of jeans and her cowboy boots. She pulled her hair into a ponytail and walked out into the night.

THE STABLES HADN'T changed since he'd first visited them as a teenager. The barn was big and cavernous, the scent of hay and sweet corn welcoming him as he stepped inside. There was a narrow aisle between the horses' stalls. Mick's horse, Rowdy—named after a TV character from a Western Mick had watched in his youth—had always had the first stall.

As a teen, Ace hadn't really appreciated being sent from Houston to some ranch out in the middle of nowhere. It had felt like the punishment it was meant to be. And he'd been just bratty and angsty enough to act like an ass for the first three months he'd been at the Bar T Ranch. But Mick kept giving him chores and allowed him the distance he needed to wake up and figure out that he'd made a mess of his life and that he was the only one who could fix it.

He walked past all of the hands' horses before he came to the few horses Mitch kept for visitors. He saddled one with the name *Carl* on its stall door. Then he found Molly's horse in the second stall. Molly had always used the stall next to her father's. And while it housed a different horse than he remembered, the wood-burned sign she'd made when she was fifteen still hung outside the door.

He heard Molly's footsteps behind him and turned to face her. He regretted leaving his bedroom when he'd heard her in the hall. She was a complication. Someone he'd never figured out how to deal with. Even from his moody, teenaged perspective there had been something about Molly Tanner that had made him want her.

"I saddled your horse," he said.

"Thanks." She took Thunder's reins and led him to the mounting block.

Ace watched the way she moved. The long easy strides that made her hips sway with each step. The denim fabric of her jeans as it pulled tight around her thighs when she mounted the horse. She settled into the saddle and then glanced over her shoulder at him. Her chestnut hair was pulled up in a high pony-tail and he couldn't take his eyes off the long sweep of her neck.

"You coming, Jason?"

He nodded. NASA trusted him with millions of dollars' worth of equipment and paid him for his opinion and his thoughts, but at this moment he knew he wasn't worth a dime. He was speechless watching this cowgirl in her element. She was at home here. Even if something happened and God forbid she lost the ranch, Molly would know who she was.

He'd never felt fully himself until he'd been above the Earth, the blue planet so beautiful at a distance and the rest of the universe spread out before him. If he was permanently grounded because of his health... who would he be? It was his goal to be part of the Cronus test missions, but that might be out of reach now.

Cronus wasn't an acronym for anything. All of the NASA missions were named for Greek gods and Cronus had been chosen for this program because he'd fallen from the sky and started a civilization on Earth, according to mythology. Many were hoping the Cronus missions and the Mars manned missions would do the same for that planet.

Before Ace had gone up to the ISS for a year, Dennis Lock, Deputy Program Manager for the Cronus mission, and Dr. Lorelei Tomlin, the team medic, had designed a fitness routine to get him ready for the long-term mission program and to see if they could counteract the expected impact of spending a year outside the Earth's gravitational field.

He'd had very little spinal-fluid loss, which was the result they had been hoping for, and he'd recovered relatively quickly from the standard loss in muscle mass, but the bone-density loss he'd suffered—and the raised calcium levels in his blood that came with it—continued to be a concern. At his medical exam Doc Tomlin had been as upset as Ace was by the unusually slow rate of improvement. He'd taken a leave to see if being away from Johnson Space Center and a different, off-site exercise regimen would help.

Osteopenia had the power to end the part of his career he loved most—actually being up in space. Something he wasn't ready for. He was determined to beat this any way he could.

He mounted Carl, and Molly touched her heels to her horse's sides and made a clicking sound, leading the way out of the barn.

The night was cool, not cold, and the sky was clear. Early May in south Texas wasn't really hot yet, at least at night. For a minute he forgot about riding and just stared at the sky. His heart took a punch and he felt a sense of fear and loss. He had to be cleared for more missions.

"You okay?" she asked.

He thought seeing the stars would remind him of who he was, but it just emphasized what was at stake.

"Yeah," he lied.

She loped along the fields past the grazing land where the cattle were kept, and he stopped thinking and just followed her.

Her ponytail flew out behind her head as she rode and it took all of his skill to keep up with her. Eventually he realized that Molly wasn't riding with him. She was racing away from something.

Her dad.

He stopped trying to keep up and let her ride as hard and fast as she could. Even though he knew there was no running away from the ghosts that were carried in one's soul.

Molly pulled up a few hundred feet in front of him and tipped her head back to the sky. He couldn't help noticing again how long and slender her neck was. Everything about her body was sleek and elegant.

When he pulled up next to her, he noticed that her eyes were wide and wet.

"I forgot how much I love to ride at night," she said.

"Me, too. It's exhilarating."

"It is. Thank you for this. I know you came here to figure out what to do with the ranch, not to deal with Mick's hot mess of a daughter."

"You're not a hot mess," he said. "I came back for you, too. We both have to decide what to do about this complicated legacy Mick left us."

"Yes," she agreed. "But not tonight."

"Definitely not," he agreed. "Where to now?"

She tipped her head back toward the stars again and he did the same. His breath caught as his eyes skimmed the sky finding what he was looking for. The International Space Station. Knowing where to look made it easy for him to spot it. He watched it moving slowly in orbit and thought of all the time he'd spent up there. He'd clocked more time than most of the other guys on his team.

"What are you looking at?"

"The space station," he said.

"Where is it?"

He lifted his arm and pointed. "It's in a slow moving orbit."

"What's it like up there?"

He shrugged. "Better men than me could probably put it into words. I just know up there…I'm free."

"Like me when I'm riding," she said, quietly.

He didn't respond, just looked up at the sky, realizing he was going to do whatever he had to in order to get mission-ready again. He wasn't done with that life. Not yet.

THEY GOT OFF their horses and left them to graze as they continued, walking. This was a side to Jason she didn't know. In fact, there was a lot to the man she had no idea about. He'd been a boy when he left to go into the military and started on his path to becoming an astronaut. And though they'd lived in the same house for a few years, they'd never had deep conversations.

Tonight she thought she finally had a glimpse of the real man.

"What's going on with you and your career?" she asked. "You said there was a medical issue."

"It's complicated."

"Which means you don't think I will understand it or you don't want to talk about it."

"You're one of the smartest women I've ever known," he said.

She smiled. "That's because I whipped your butt at AP calculus back in the day."

"I'm a little better at it now," he admitted.

"And I never have to use it. Ironic, isn't it?"

"Life is complicated," he said. "Way more so than we ever could have guessed in high school."

"True. So you don't want to talk about your health and I can respect that, but I need to know if you are in danger. We're a good forty-five minutes from the nearest hospital."

"I'm okay," he said. "It's not anything that's going to kill me while I'm here."

Health concerns.

He'd said it like that because he didn't want to talk about it and make it seem more real. Giving it a name would mean he was fighting something serious. Instead of, say, a cold or a muscle strain. Those were things anyone could beat. This? He wasn't sure. But being purposely vague would just make it seem more mysterious to her and he doubted she'd leave it alone.

"I have some symptoms of spaceflight osteopenia."

"I don't know what that is," Molly said. "But it sounds like osteoporosis. Does it have something to do with your bones?"

"Yes. In microgravity, astronauts don't put weight

on our back or leg muscles, and the longer we're up there the more they start to weaken and get smaller."

"Have you lost height?" she asked.

He shrugged. "When I first returned to Earth I was a bit taller, but now I'm back to normal. They are more concerned with my raised calcium levels and loss of bone density."

"What can you do?" she asked.

"I'm doing it—or I will be, at least. Working on the ranch, lifting, putting my body to good use, all of these things are going to help," he said with more than a bit of hope and bravado. "I'm supposed to be tested again in three months. I did an advanced regimen during my time on the ISS and if Doctor Tomlin's theories are correct I should improve more quickly than others have in the past. Part of my mission on the ISS was for her to test the effects of prolonged exposure to space. She has me trying different exercises and a special diet to decrease my recovery time."

Molly nodded. He'd shared his medical information but hadn't really told her what that meant to him.

"How long are you going to stay?" she asked. She needed to know. She needed to make plans. That was what she should be doing instead of walking in the moonlight with Jason McCoy. But here she was.

"It's three months to my reevaluation. That should give us some time to figure out what to do with the ranch."

"I don't want to sell it," she said. "And I can't buy you out. Not now."

"Oh. I was really hoping to sell my half to you. My life isn't here at the Bar T."

"Dad borrowed some money from you, so you must

know the ranch isn't as profitable as it once was," she said.

"I could just sign over my half to you. NASA pays me well enough, and by rights the ranch should be yours."

That idea didn't sit right with her. After all, he'd already put money into the ranch and never got a cent back. "No. Thank you for the offer, but Dad wanted you to have this for a reason. He wouldn't have felt right not paying you back, at least. And even though I don't understand or appreciate why he made us full partners in this ranch, I won't go against his wishes. Maybe you will find that you like the ranching life." Every once in a while the breeze blew in the right direction and the scent of his aftershave wafted on the wind.

"I don't think I will." He stared up at the stars again, looking as if he would fly up to them now if he could and leave everything earthbound behind.

"There's a lot more to you than I remember," he said. "Though, to be fair, I don't remember much except that you could outride me."

"Fair enough," she said. "All I remember was that I really wanted to kiss you and you were determined not to get involved with me."

He laughed.

She watched him a second and then smiled. It was the first time since her dad's death that she'd felt... happy.

He noticed her watching him and raised one eyebrow at her.

"You made me smile."

"I'm glad," he said. "I like your smile."

"You do?"

"Yes, ma'am."

She shook her head. "How many women have fallen for your 'aw shucks' routine?"

"A fair few," he admitted with a sheepish smile. "Not everyone is impressed with my being an astronaut and having stayed on the ISS."

"Really?" she asked. It gave her the shivers to think of the things he'd done and seen. "I am."

"You are?"

"I've only left the state of Texas once and that was just to go to Louisiana to pick up a bull Dad had purchased. So you having left the planet *is* a big deal," she said, wondering who would disagree.

He stopped walking and turned to look at her. His features weren't clear in the darkness, but she felt his attention on her.

She licked her lips and tried to step back because she was a hot mess, as she'd said earlier. And Jason was feeling uncertain and worried about his future. This was the worst possible time to be kissing him. And more—she wanted more.

She knew that.

She'd been alone for too long. It had been over eighteen months since she'd ended her last relationship and most of the time she was just fine getting her romance fix on television or in books. But tonight, standing out here in the moonlight with him, she craved...something more.

She never gave in to impulses. That was a lie—she had tonight. She'd left her room, gone into the hallway. He'd kissed her. And when their lips had met... she'd changed.

Something fundamental had shifted inside of her and she was honest enough to admit she didn't know how to react to it. She should never have kissed Jason. She should have left him in the past, in those teenage-girl dreams.

But he was here and that kiss was fresh in her mind. Her lips tingled and she realized that being this close to him stirred something inside of her that she usually did a good job of ignoring. Stirred the passion and the desire that she preferred to think she was the master of. That she had been able to control until Jason.

"Jason..."

"Yes?"

"Why did you stop walking?" she asked.

"Because I wanted to show you this," he said. He drew her into his arms and she started to lift her face to his, her eyes slowly closing. But he turned her so that he stood behind her and put his hand under her chin, tipping her head back toward the sky.

She was on fire with need. But he treated her like a friend.

They were friends.

Just friends.

She repeated that over and over again as he pointed to the stars. Was the passion she felt one-sided?

3

ACE KEPT HIS touch light on her chin as he tipped her head up to the sky. He wanted more. Hell, she was more addicting than his first taste of flying Mach 1 had been. But he wasn't back for good and she deserved more than a summer fling.

He had always loved the stars and the sky but, more than that, the freedom they had represented. He knew life had been different for Molly. She'd had her dad and when her mom had passed she'd had Rina. She'd grown up in a house filled with love and support. He hadn't. He'd wanted to escape and run as far away from Texas as he could get.

Ironic that he'd ended up finding his home in Houston. He'd thought he'd have to leave that city far behind to find peace, but he'd been wrong. It wasn't the first thing he'd been wrong about and he doubted very much it would be the last.

"What am I looking at?" she asked. Her voice was soft like the gentle breeze stirring around them and her hair smelled of summer strawberries. He remembered the way it had looked falling in disheveled waves around her shoulders and was tempted to remove the elastic holding it in place now.

"Venus," he said. "Venus takes only a fraction of one Earth year—225 days—to orbit the sun once, so we see it frequently in the night sky. Sometimes Jupiter and Mars line up with it—it's rare, but you can see all three in a triangle in the sky."

"Now?"

"No. Usually closer to sunrise," he said.

"What's it like to see the sunrise from orbit?"

He wasn't sure he could put it into words. He wasn't one of those poetic guys who turned their adventures on the space station into books. Despite his time with NASA, he was still more of a cowboy, he guessed, even if he didn't want to be tied to the Earth.

"It's awesome," he said at last.

She chuckled.

"Awesome?"

"Yeah, got a problem with that?"

"Not at all," she said. "Good to know that you haven't changed all that much."

For a moment he didn't follow and then he remembered when he'd first come to the ranch. All he'd said to everything was *awesome* in a sarcastic tone.

"Forgot about that. I don't use the word much anymore. Must be something about the Bar T that brings it out in me."

"Must be," she said, stepping aside. "I guess we should think about heading back."

"If you do, you'll miss the best part."

"What's the best part?" she asked, turning in his arms. She had her head tipped back and their eyes met in the inky darkness. It was hard to read the expression in hers and that made him feel a bit freer. She wouldn't be able to read the expression in his eyes, either. He didn't want her to see how much she affected him.

He traced one finger down the line of her neck. "You are so delicate-looking in the moonlight. Like the Carina Nebula."

"I've never heard of it," she said. Her words were soft, and he had the feeling she was waiting for something.

Him?

"It's not as well-known as many of the other nebulas. It's found in the southern sky."

"South like southern hemisphere?"

"Yeah. Remember how I wasn't sure where Montana was for the longest time?" he asked. He'd been so green when he'd lived here. When he was surviving on the streets, the only things that had mattered were food and staying away from the authorities. He'd never done well in school until he'd come to the Bar T and hadn't had those worries anymore.

"I do. But you always knew the night sky," she said. "Was it because of… I don't know much about your family. Dad always respected the privacy of the guys who came here. Said if you wanted me to know your story, you'd tell me."

"Nothing to tell. I knew the sky because I read a book when I was younger, before things got rough, about sailors who navigated using the stars. It just sort of stuck."

"Probably like me and *Misty of Chincoteague*. If I hadn't already loved horses, that book made me."

He didn't dwell on the past, especially his childhood. There was nothing but pain and humiliation there and the future had always been where he'd seen himself. But he realized now how much of the man he was today had been shaped by those events. He was a maverick, even in the Cronus program. Always pushing boundaries and going on missions that others thought twice about. It was why his boss was determined that he get back in top physical condition as quickly as possible.

He was realistic enough to know he probably wouldn't be part of the Mars mission team since the first one wouldn't likely happen for at least another twenty years. The test missions, though. The long-term journeys and a possible moon base. Those were all programs he was interested in.

But Cronus was close to his dream mission. They'd be taking up the components for the first base between Earth and Mars. They'd establish the way station and each mission would continue to test human endurance in space.

"Like that," he agreed. But he wasn't thinking about their conversation anymore. He was thinking about Molly. And how she'd always been just out of his reach. He had been afraid he wasn't good enough for her as a teenager, and he realized now that he'd also been running from anything that hinted at a normal life. Still was.

But in the moonlight, with the horses neighing behind them, it was easy to see that none of that mattered. He cupped the back of her head and lowered his mouth to hers. Slowly, in case she wanted to pull back. But she didn't.

She rose on her tiptoes and put her hands on his shoulders. She held him loosely for balance and he felt the brush of her breath over his lips a second before their mouths met. He moved his lips over hers and closed his eyes.

He knew he couldn't stay, that this could never be more than a few moonlight kisses, but somehow that seemed perfect to him.

THROWING CAUTION TO the wind wasn't her MO, but this was Jason. And she knew no matter what happened with his health, he wouldn't stay here on the Bar T Ranch for long. He had always been destined for bigger things.

She sighed and almost let her thoughts derail her, but then she shook her head. Shook herself. Not tonight. Like she'd promised herself earlier this evening when she left her bed...no regrets.

Pushing her fingers into his hair, cupping his scalp, she tilted her head to the side to deepen the kiss. Now that they had been out here riding and talking, he tasted different to her. More like adventure and the promise of things she'd never be brave enough to take for herself.

He tasted like a man who was leaving, the same way he had that long-ago summer when she'd wanted to be sophisticated enough to seduce him into staying.

She pulled back.

"What is it?"

How could she tell him that suddenly she felt too silly, too foolish for him? She couldn't. She wouldn't. "Nothing."

"Dammit, Molly. It's just a kiss," he said, his Texas drawl stronger than it had been earlier.

It couldn't lead anywhere—that was the problem.

Opportunities for real, lasting romance were lacking in this town and maybe she was tired of it. There weren't a lot of men in Cole's Hill that she would consider dating. Mainly because they were either ranchers like herself and busy with their own land, or she'd dated them in high school, or they weren't her type. And she was here with Jason…Ace. It was hard to think of him as Ace.

"You'd think that I could just let go and have some mindless fun, but even now, with nothing left to lose, I can't do it."

He pulled her into his arms and hugged her. Just held her close. She wasn't crying like she had been earlier. That flood of tears thankfully wasn't near the surface. But the loneliness she'd felt lately, as she'd come to accept that her dad was truly gone, was back.

She turned her head to the side, rested her cheek against his chest and listened to his heartbeat. It was strong. Steady.

"Just once I want to be like one of those brash women on TV who takes what she wants and smiles as she resumes her normal life."

"Aw, Molly," Jason said, tipping her back and dropping a sweet, butterfly kiss on the end of her nose. "That's not you."

"More's the pity," she said.

He rubbed his thumb over her jawbone. His hands were firm but not rough. Not like hers, calloused and hardened from years of working with cattle and the land. As he touched her a slow heat began to burn deep inside. A shiver went from her jaw to her neck, then over her shoulder and down her arm. Her lips parted.

As Jason stared down at her, she wished she could

read the expression in his eyes. She couldn't tell what he was thinking, and she didn't want to do something…what? Dumb? Too late. It had been too late since the moment her father's attorney had revealed that she and Jason were jointly inheriting the Bar T. It had been too late since she'd realized he would be coming back and something feminine and needy had awoken inside of her.

She stared up at him, his eyes silvery pools in the dim light, and realized that she was a coward. All this wanting to be someone else wasn't true to her. She was hiding because she was afraid.

She was twenty-nine. Well past the age when she'd thought she'd let fear drive her. She felt the wash of his breath over her and she closed her eyes—somehow everything seemed easier with her eyes closed. Then she felt his thumb rub over her bottom lip.

She sighed again.

He pulled her more fully against him, her breasts resting on his chest and their hips lightly touching. She felt the brush of his lips over hers. The intimacy of it heightened because the only senses she used at this moment were taste and touch. His body heat surrounded her. His arms were strong as he held her close.

His lips were warm and firm, and as he opened them over hers she let go and just experienced Jason. The way his tongue brushed hers slowly and then pulled back. The way he kept one hand gently on her shoulder, his finger stroking the pulse at the curve where her neck and shoulder met. The way he let the kiss develop between them with no rush or agenda.

She felt safe.

She felt like they could stand there all night rediscovering each other and the passion she'd been too young to really understand all those years ago.

She rubbed her tongue over his and he moaned a little, shifting her stance. He put one of his hands on her back and drew her even closer so that she was nestled in the cradle of his legs. He cupped her butt, caressing it through her jeans, and she shivered as sensation washed through her.

She put her hands on his hips, holding him as much to steady herself as to feel him. He was solid, muscled. And for the first time since he'd set foot back on the Bar T, she acknowledged that she wanted him, needed him to stay right here with her. But she knew he never would.

MOLLY FELT SO GOOD. He didn't have a lot of time in his life for romance. He dated—well, if one-night stands and vacation flings could be called dating—but he had dreams that no woman could compete with. That had been true for longer than he could remember.

But Molly tempted him. She wasn't casual—no matter how much he wanted to pretend otherwise. And he was tied to her and to this land until they could come up with a solution that would satisfy them both.

Then there was his health. He glanced up at the starry sky again and then cursed and closed his eyes. There was no place to run from this.

And at the moment Molly was the only thing that felt real to him.

He put his hands on her face. Felt the softness of her skin. The scent of her perfume surrounded him and his eyes drifted closed as he let go. Really let go of everything.

Her lips were soft under his, pliant. Her tongue rubbed over his and he sucked it gently into his mouth. One of his hands left her head and moved down her back, his fingers testing the resilience of her hips.

He groaned at the way her curves fit against him. It was as if she was custom-made for him the way his space suit was. He shifted back, lifting her off her feet.

She clung to him as she tipped her head and her tongue plunged deeper into his mouth. He hardened in a rush, rocking his hips forward until his erection was nestled at the top of her thighs.

Her legs parted and she wrapped them around his hips. He staggered backward and then realized there was nothing to lean against. He carefully knelt down and lowered Molly to the ground beneath him. He braced one hand on the soft grass and shifted so that he straddled her.

She turned her head to the side.

"My ponytail is uncomfortable," she said.

He reached beneath her head and pulled out the elastic. Burying his fingers in her thick hair, he fanned it out around her head.

He stretched out next to her on the grass and drew her up on her side so that they faced each other.

"There's an easier way to do this, but I wanted to see your hair down," he said.

"Why?" she asked, her voice was quiet, shy almost.

Not the Molly who could tame a wild horse or quell an ornery ranch hand with just a glance. This was the woman he'd always wondered about. The one who sometimes wandered into his dreams before he sent her on her way.

"It's beautiful." He rubbed a few strands between his thumb and forefinger.

"No. It's nothing special. Just sort of average."

In her words he heard the implicit belief that *she* was average. And that shook him because she'd always been anything but.

"You know you're not average," he said.

"I think for this area of the country I am."

"Nah, you stand out, Molly Tanner. You always have. Your eyes are like dark chocolate—a man could lose himself staring into those eyes—and your hair… it's so silky and soft and I just want to bury my face in and breathe in the sweet strawberry scent."

She stared at him. He wondered where the words were coming from, as well. Was he saying this because of the moonlight? Because for the first time in his entire life he had no idea what he was doing next and getting lost in Molly seemed like as good a path as any?

God, he really hoped not.

She watched him with eyes that asked too many questions he couldn't answer, so he took her mouth in a kiss that was deep and filled with passion. That left no room for thinking—for either of them.

He pulled her into the curve of his body, felt her drape her thigh over his top leg and he nestled his throbbing cock against the center of her body.

The night deepened around them and still they lay there in the grass, kissing and caressing until his horse wandered over and nudged him in the back. He sat up and Molly sat up next to him.

It was too soon to take this any further. They were business partners…maybe friends…and sex wasn't the best idea to keep things uncomplicated.

"I guess we should be heading back," she said.

"Yeah. We don't want to be out here when the hands start riding the fence and moving the cattle."

"Definitely not."

He helped her to her feet and they both brushed themselves off. She bit her lower lip and looked over at him. Questions, he saw them again in her eyes.

"Thank you for riding with me," he said to divert her.

She was stubborn, and for a minute he didn't think it had worked. But in the end she just nodded. "No problem."

They rode back to the barn in silence and both of them stabled their horses without saying a word. He wasn't as practiced as Molly and when he looked up from putting away his tack she was gone.

Gone.

It was probably for the best. But he already missed her.

4

MOLLY WASN'T HAVING the best day. Jason had left a message with Jeb that he was going to camp out on the land that evening and that he'd meet her at the lawyer's office the next day. A horse had reared when she'd been trying to saddle it and its hoof had come down hard on her booted foot. She was pretty sure she had a deep bruise and hoped there were no broken bones.

So when she rounded the house and saw the big late-model Ford Bronco sitting in the circular drive she almost turned around and walked back to the barn.

The last person she wanted to talk to this afternoon was Wil Abernathy.

But the driver's-side door opened before she could leave and she wouldn't give him the impression she was running away.

"Afternoon, Molly," Wil said as she came closer.

Wil was five years older than her and about as tall as Jason's six-foot frame. He'd spent his life on his family's ranch and the years had been good to him. Their derricks were still pulling oil from the ground and the Abernathys ran one of the largest and most successful stud farms and insemination programs in the country.

Wil was okay. A little too slick for her taste. The girls she'd gone to school with in Cole's Hill had always said Wil, with his thick blond hair and blue eyes, looked like Brad Pitt. He had on his dress jeans—she could tell because they were dark blue denim and not faded at all—hand-tooled boots and a Stetson. All the Abernathy men wore Stetsons.

"Afternoon, Wil. What can I do for you?"

"I'm here to sweeten the offer I made your father," he said. "Maybe we could go inside and discuss it?"

"I'm fine right here."

"Damn. You are just as stubborn as your dad was," he said. "I was sorry to hear about his death."

"Thank you. Thank you, also, for the flowers you sent. I noticed you and your sister at the funeral service, as well."

"Mick was a good guy and, despite the fact that he didn't get along with my dad, I never had any problems with him."

"He was a good guy," Molly agreed. "I'm not selling."

"You haven't heard my proposal yet," Wil said.

"Okay. Tell me," she said. Sweat was dripping down the back of her neck and she felt every inch the working cowgirl talking to Wil. If she hadn't been so determined to keep him out of her house, she could be inside drinking iced tea in the air-conditioning. But her father had always said no Abernathy would set foot in the house...and she was honoring that.

"I want to lease some of your land for grazing," he

said. "Damn, it's hot. Want to sit in my Bronco if we can't go inside?"

She shook her head. "Do you know why Dad was so insistent on keeping you and your kin out of the house?"

"I'm not entirely sure, but I think it has something to do with your mom," Wil said. "My pops just said that the Tanners were sore winners."

It was another story she'd never know since she hadn't thought to ask her dad about it, really push him to tell her what had happened. But she was hot and tired and Wil was here offering her an olive branch.

"Why don't you have a seat on the east-facing porch? There are ceiling fans and we get a nice breeze from the creek. I'll get us something cold to drink."

"Sounds good," Wil said.

Molly heard him walking behind her as they went up the steps and she gestured to the right so he knew where to go. "Do you mind if I change out of these clothes?"

"Take your time. I scheduled the entire afternoon to be out here."

"Thank you."

She opened the front door and as she closed it behind her she tipped her head back and let the air-conditioning sweep over her. "Rina!"

"Yeah?"

"Wil is on the east porch. Will you bring him some iced tea?"

Rina poked her head out of the kitchen and looked down the hall at her. "Abernathy?"

"Yes. Be nice. He's got an offer to lease some land.

It might be the cash influx we need to bail ourselves out of this mess."

"What about Ace?" Rina said, wiping her hands on her apron as she walked toward Molly.

"What about him?" Molly asked. "He's not here and Wil is. I'm going to take the fastest shower in history and be right back down."

Rina patted her shoulder as Molly sort of limped by her. "Okay, sunshine. I'll keep him entertained until you come back down."

"Thanks," Molly said, walking past Rina up the stairs. She felt that urge to cry again. Not because of the pain or the situation but because her dad wasn't here. She wanted to know what had happened between him and Wil's father. Was she betraying him by even agreeing to listen to Wil's proposal?

But he wasn't there. She showered off the day and felt better for it. She pulled on a denim skirt and a sleeveless top then put on her flip-flops, inspecting the bruise on the top of her left foot. Pulling her hair into a ponytail, she went out to the porch where Wil waited for her.

He had a slice of lemon icebox pie and a half-empty glass of iced tea next to him on the table.

"Okay, Abernathy, tell me about this idea of yours," she said as she sat down.

He leaned back in the rocking chair. "My sister wants to raise Scottish Highland cattle. It's a small herd and I'd like to keep them separate from our stock and the bulls. Leasing the grazing rights to your land—the section that borders our ranch—would allow me to do that."

He told her more about his plan and what he would

pay. She took his proposal, which he'd thoughtfully typed up for her, and told him she'd get back to him with an answer in a few days. The deposit he offered wouldn't be enough to clear their debt, but it would put a nice dent in it.

It was an option she should definitely consider. Actually, it was probably the best option she had right now.

She couldn't help but think that she might have liked Wil if there wasn't a family feud between them. He was a nice guy. Solid. The kind of man who knew what ranch life demanded and was happy to live it.

Not like Jason. *Ace*, she reminded herself.

Molly put the file in her office. She kept looking out the window, hoping to see Jason come walking up, but he wasn't going to. He'd made a point of putting distance between them after the intimacy of last night. She knew she had to give up the idea that he was going to ride to the rescue. She was on her own.

DINNER HAD BEEN a loud affair with the hands all giving their opinions on what she should do with the ranch. It was going to affect all of them and she thought they should know that the ranch was in financial trouble. Even though she wanted to ensure their jobs, there would have to be changes. Jeb was the quietest man she knew and he'd just sat there listening to all the ideas. Most of the men weren't too keen on a dude ranch and if Molly was being totally honest, she wasn't, either. She didn't want to have to cater to people on vacation.

"I'm just out of ideas," she said at last.

"Something will come to you," Jeb said. "It always does. In the meantime, I'm going to put some of the hands on land clearing. The acres down at the edge of our property haven't been touched for a while and we should get them in shape for whatever you decide to do."

"Thanks, Jeb."

He nodded.

"Also, Dad left the ranch to both me and Jason McCoy. So he might be around over the next few months as we are figuring out what to do," she said. No use pretending the decision was just hers, even if it did feel that way. She'd called Rupert's office earlier and he'd made it clear that the will stipulated she and Jason had to make any decisions for selling or changing the purpose of the ranch land together.

"He's a little rusty, but I think he might make a decent hand eventually," one of them said.

Guffaws of laughter spread around the table.

"He might. He lived here as a teenager," Molly said, once the laughter died down. "We used to run a last-chance program for troubled boys. They came from Houston mainly, but we got some from Dallas. Dad and Jeb were in charge."

"Given how much hell Mick and I raised together, we figured we'd be good examples for straightening those boys out," Jeb said.

"You were," Rina added. "All of them have gone on to do good things."

"Is that a possibility?" Jeb asked after the hands had finished eating and left to do their evening chores. "Do you want to take boys in again?"

"No. I'm not like Dad. I don't have the strength to do that," she said, getting to her feet and helping Rina clear the dishes.

"Fair enough. Just let me know what you want me to do," Jeb said.

"I will. Thanks."

"Girl, you know you're like a daughter to me. You don't have to thank me for doing what family does for each other," Jeb said, giving her a quick hug on his way out the door.

Family.

The word had always been unspoken in the house. Aside from her and her dad, there wasn't a blood bond between any of the other residents of the Bar T Ranch, but they'd always felt like a family. Even Jason, when he had lived there.

"What's up?" Rina asked.

"Nothing."

"Liar," Rina said. "I've got a bottle of pinot noir that my sister sent for my birthday. Meet me on the deck."

"Rina—"

"I'm not taking no for an answer. If you don't want to talk, that's fine. But you've been alone enough today and you still haven't found the answers you're searching for."

"You're right."

"I know," Rina said with a wink.

Molly just shook her head and walked out onto the deck that she and her dad had weatherproofed at the beginning of last summer. It was slightly raised, looking down over the large kidney-shaped pool. She walked to the sturdy pine railing and stood there looking out over the land.

The Tanners had been given these 760 acres in a land grant from the Spanish King back in the 1800s. For as far as she could see, the land was hers. They'd run cattle from the beginning and had found oil in the '60s. They'd had several wells that had produced a nice income during her grandparents' lifetime, but by the time Molly was born they weren't producing as much. Her kingdom wasn't what it used to be. Well, hers and Jason's. She liked the view. She liked that she could see the pastures where the cattle were kept and the barn where the horses were stabled. She liked that beyond the pastures and buildings was land that hadn't been developed or used for anything other than ranching and drilling.

Her heart ached at the thought of all she was facing. She needed her dad back, just for a few minutes so she could ask him what the hell he'd been thinking when he'd left half of the ranch to Jason. *Why?* She knew he had to have some kind of motive, but for the life of her it kept eluding her. The value of the land was so far beyond the debt they owed Jason.

The sun started to sink a little lower toward the horizon and the automatic outdoor lights kicked on as Rina walked out with the wine, a couple of glasses and a cheese tray. Hidden bug zappers under the deck kept the mosquitos at bay. She walked over to the seating area where two lounge chairs sat next to a low side table.

"Thanks for suggesting this," Molly said as she took her first sip.

"I needed it, too."

She was just now realizing she hadn't been the best friend to Rina recently. She'd been too caught up in trying to keep moving so she didn't break down. She reached across the expanse and squeezed her friend's arm. "I'm sorry I haven't been chatty lately."

"It's all right. You needed time to get used to things. So did I, but I was just feeling a little lonely. We haven't had a girls' night in a while and I figured if I was feeling it you definitely had to be, too."

"I am. There are too many men here," Molly said. "You know what I mean?"

"I don't think that's the problem. I think you're more bothered by the one man who wasn't at dinner."

"I am," she said, taking another sip of her wine.

"What happened between you two last night?"

"Nothing. Just a kiss."

"A kiss. Want to talk about it?"

"No," she said, fidgeting with the glass. "Maybe. It was nothing. But then it felt like something more. I sound like an idiot."

"Men do that," she said.

"Really? I've never known a man to do this to me."

"Some men affect us like that," Rina said. "The ones who change us."

"Who affected you that way?" Molly asked, not wanting to believe that Jason could change her. She liked who she was.

"Never you mind," Rina said. "I met him before I came out here to live with you. And his life kept him in Houston."

"You could go to Houston, you know?"

"We're both of us too stubborn to change," Rina said.

Molly hoped she wasn't like that, but she had a feeling she was.

They didn't talk about men anymore that night. Just sipped their wine and watched the sunset. But Jason was on her mind and she suspected that Rina was thinking of the man in Houston. She realized that relationships were never easy and the thought brought her no comfort at all.

MOLLY STOPPED BY Jammin' Java for a mocha latte the next morning. It was busy…well, as busy as a coffeehouse in a small town could be. She saw all the usual customers and they nodded and called out hellos to her.

Maybe it was the fact that Jason had awakened something in her when he'd kissed her—forgotten memories of a life she might have had—or perhaps it was because her father had died, but she had a sense that her life was never going to be more than this. That whenever she came into town for the next fifty years, it would play out just the same.

That thought used to bring her ease. Reminded her that she knew who she was and where she belonged. But that kiss with Jason under the stars two nights ago had stirred something inside of her. Something she wasn't too sure would ever go back to sleep.

Lacey Duvall looked up from behind the counter and smiled when Molly walked up.

"Mocha latte?"

"Yeah."

"I heard Jason McCoy is back in town," Lacey said in a questioning sort of way. The two of them had dated a couple of times in high school. Maybe she was hoping to see him again.

"He inherited half of the Bar T. So he's here to take care of that," Molly said. "Then he's going back to Houston."

"You okay with that?" Lacey asked, turning to the back counter and grabbing Molly's coffee from her teenaged assistant. "He's been gone a dog's age and you haven't heard from him before now, have you?"

Lacey was a gossip, though not in a malicious way. Molly supposed it would happen to anyone who worked in a small-town coffee shop.

"It was a surprise," Molly admitted. She smiled and nodded at the kid as she took her coffee from Lacey. "But of course I'm going to honor Dad's wishes."

The bell on the coffeehouse door pinged and Lacey turned to greet her next customer with a smile.

"Jason McCoy, I wondered if you were going to stop by," Lacey said.

Molly stepped over to the bar to add a packet of sugar to her latte and then stirred it slowly. Way slower than was called for.

"I heard this place had the best coffee in town and had to check it out," Jason said. When he'd left thirteen years ago it hadn't yet opened.

"It's the only coffee in town so I guess you are right," Lacey said. "What'll it be?"

"Hey, Lacey. Good to see you again. Filtered coffee, please. The biggest cup you have."

Molly glanced over her shoulder at him. She wanted to play it cool. It was probably no big deal to him to make out with her, but it was a big deal to her. She realized just how limiting her life had been staying here. If she'd gone out and seen the world…maybe she wouldn't be so fascinated by his damned blue eyes and firm mouth.

He stepped closer and looked down at her, a furrow wrinkling his brow.

"What?"

"I asked how you were," he said.

"Good. I'd like to discuss a few ideas about the ranch. Maybe we can do that before we head over to see Rupert."

"Okay. You want to talk here or in the park? It's a nice day and I saw an empty bench on my way in."

"Park sounds good to me," she said. That way the town gossips—and, let's face it, in a town this size everyone knew each other's business—couldn't hear what they were saying. Hell, it didn't matter what they said—people were always going to talk. Many of them probably remembered how she'd followed Jason around town the summer before he left. How she'd tried wearing makeup and short skirts to catch his attention…

He called out a good-bye to Lacey. Molly noticed Lacey had her cell phone in her hand, furiously texting something…probably about them. She was embarrassed and a little bit…well…excited that she was being linked to Jason. And that was the problem right there.

He wanted her to buy him out or have her accept his offer to turn over his half of the ranch so he could leave. Go back to Houston. And the truth was she wanted him to stay.

They walked over to the park bench. She sat down on one end. Jason stood there for a minute then stooped to put his coffee on the ground by her foot. He stayed there so that they were at eye level and she looked at him.

"What are you doing?"

"Trying to see what's going on in your pretty head," he said.

"Don't."

"Don't what?"

"Try to be charming," she said. "Sit down and let's talk about the ranch. That's all we have between us."

"We have a hell of a lot more than that."

"Passion?" she asked, remembering the other night. "Dad always said passion leads to trouble."

"And he was right. But not this time," Jason said, putting his hand on her leg. "Are you ticked at me again?"

She shook her head. "Just unsure and kind of mad at myself. It was one thing to have a crush on you way back then, but as a woman I should know better."

"Better than what?"

"Than to fall for you," she said. She took a sip of her coffee and looked away from him. Across the street she saw a group of elementary school students all walking in a row and she knew they were heading to the library because it was Tuesday and that's what they did on Tuesday. They had probably been doing it since the library opened back in 1915.

"Hell," he said. "You want to do this here?"

"You're the one who started it," she said. She hated it, but he brought out her competitive side. Why did she need to one-up him all the time? she wondered. She probably needed to stop reacting to everything he said. But she wasn't sure she could.

"I am. Well, fine, I needed to get out of the house for the night because you made me want to knock on your bedroom door. I thought, hey, if I am grounded from NASA, maybe this life wouldn't be too bad, and you know what?" he asked, pausing.

"What?" she asked after the pause lengthened.

"That wasn't right. I was using you as an excuse to settle. And you deserve better from me than that."

Settling...it made sense, but it still hurt. She closed her eyes. Cole's Hill was where he went to escape from his problems. She didn't want to be an escape for him. She wanted him in her life because he wanted to be there. Not because he felt trapped and out of choices.

"Fair enough. You gave me time to think as well," she said.

"Yeah, what about?"

"That I don't want to be a fling for you. Your summer romance before you head back to NASA."

"You think I'll be going back?"

She nodded. "I've never seen you lose anything you really wanted." She stood and carefully stepped around him. "I'll meet you over at Rupert's."

5

JASON WATCHED MOLLY walk away and let her go. He had been honest, but the fact was their situation was complicated and he hadn't done either one of them any favors by leaving the house for the night because she'd gotten too close. He'd justified it to himself, but then he was good at doing that. He spent a lot of time alone with his thoughts. Training to be an astronaut, spending as many days orbiting Earth as he had—it gave a man time to think.

Time to know himself better than most would be comfortable with. But he'd always been one to keep his thoughts to himself and he'd done that as he'd watched her walk away from the bench. As he'd realized the ranch had a pull on his soul that he'd never known was there.

It wasn't as strong as the call to explore the universe. But the call was there all the same. And he'd felt a tearing deep inside where he'd always been so sure that nothing could rock him.

A need. A desire for Molly and something that only

she could offer him. He'd kept his distance last night because she called to him.

No other woman would tempt him to give up his place in NASA—to give up his dream—but there was a part of him that knew she did.

And he couldn't justify sleeping with her...having that summer affair she was so afraid of. But he knew if they were near each other it would happen.

They wanted each other. Those kinds of sparks wouldn't be denied for long. His will would weaken and then...

Stop.

He had to stop trying to control everything. To know every outcome. He was trying to manage Molly as if she was a mission, but he couldn't be objective. He didn't think there was a man alive who could be objective about a pair of hips and legs that looked that good. He grabbed his coffee and followed her.

He put his hand on her shoulder and she turned, her long chestnut hair brushing his skin. Her hair was soft, like the cashmere lining his leather gloves. And he wanted to grab one of the tendrils and wrap it around his finger, but he didn't.

"I don't want to screw up," he said and felt better for it. "I want to make sure I don't hurt either of us."

"Life's not like that," she said at last. "I appreciate it, but you can't do that."

"I know. I think that's why I've spent so much time up there." He looked at the sky. "Up there I am never distracted from the mission. I always know what to do...but with you it's never been like that."

"For me, neither. Listen, I know the timing is wrong

for this…" She gestured at the two of them and then shrugged.

He laughed. "I have no idea what to call it, either."

"Flames," she said. "It feels like a fire inside of me and I have no idea how to put it out."

"Fire is dangerous for an astronaut," he said.

"For a cowgirl, too," she said. "So let's be smart."

"I want to," he admitted, but then he touched her neck, just ran his finger along the column of her throat, and a jolt went up his arm as she shivered.

A light pink flush spread from the skin showing above the scooped top of her dress up her neck, and her lips parted as she went stock-still.

"We can't be smart with this between us," he said, softly. He leaned in, putting his forehead on hers and looked into those beautiful brown eyes. "Can we?"

She closed her eyes and licked her lips. "I don't know. I can't think when you touch me."

"I have an idea," he said, stepping back and dropping his hand. He had a hard time thinking of anything other than the way she'd felt in his arms the other night. The way she had tasted. Had a woman ever tasted as good as Molly? He couldn't think of one.

"Yeah?"

"We just see what happens. Spend our days together on the ranch and see if this is more than just lust. Neither one of us are casual people. We aren't going to just fall into bed because it feels good."

"I'm not too sure about that," she said in a wry tone that made him smile.

Damn.

He liked her.

That was why he needed to make sure he didn't hurt

her. He could do this. They were friends and now co-owners of a ranch—one that would require plenty of work if they wanted to get it back on solid financial footing. He couldn't screw this up.

He had to imagine he was definitely going back to NASA, though. He couldn't let Molly be his contingency plan, his life, if he was denied a place on the Cronus program. He knew that. He wanted to believe he wouldn't use Molly in that way. But a part of him, the part that had been a loser before he came to the Bar T Ranch as a teenager, wasn't too sure. That part of him wanted to just take what he needed.

"This isn't your average will and you could probably contest it and get a judge to set aside Mick's wishes. But, Molly, he was your dad and, Jason, I know you two were close. This is more about respecting his wishes than upholding the law. If you take it to court, it'll be a long time before either of you can do anything with the ranch."

Molly crossed her legs. She'd worn a sleeveless dress that fell loosely over her body, accentuating the strength in her arms and her long legs. Her boots were hand-tooled and had turquoise accents in the leatherwork. She'd pulled the top of her hair back but left the rest to hang around her shoulders.

Maybe that was why he'd been doing all that soul baring in the middle of town—he was thinking with his boner instead of his head.

"Okay. Do we need to do anything to move forward?" Molly asked. "Legally?"

"You both have to sign off on any move to improve the ranch or change its purpose. That includes selling off or leasing part of it. I have the paperwork all ready to go. You can fill it in and both sign it and I'll witness it."

"We haven't had a chance to discuss what we want to do," Ace said.

Running the Bar T wasn't part of his plans for the future. He figured he'd recuperate here, do his exercise regimen, maybe stoke the flames of the fire between himself and Molly and leave after his three months' leave. But this was…complicated.

"I figured as much. If you want to, you can use my conference room to discuss plans. If it's going to take longer than a few hours, we can schedule another day for you to come back."

"I'd like to get this sorted out today," Molly said, leaning forward to take the papers Rupert held out to them. "The ranch can't wait any longer. We need to make some decisions to ensure the financial future of the Bar T."

"I agree. I don't want to wait," Jason said. "Where is the conference room?"

"Last door on the right. Just let Shirley know when you are done and I'll get the paperwork witnessed and notarized."

"Thanks," Molly said.

They stood at the same time. Molly slung her leather bag over her shoulder and turned toward the door. Jason put his hand at the small of her back and reached around her to open it.

He led her down the hall. Once they were in the conference room, she stepped away from him, putting her bag down on the table.

She didn't sit but walked over to the window at the

end of the room that looked out at the street. It was a quiet business street that bordered the park. He stayed where he was, unsure what she was thinking.

"The situation is really very bleak. I've got a couple hundred head of cattle and we'll make a profit but not nearly enough to pay back the money you lent us or the loan Dad took out to cover some investment losses. I don't know if he had a plan to get out of the hole, but…I have a few thoughts," she said, finally turning to face him.

She was serious. She looked like the same country girl he'd been talking to all morning, but in her eyes he saw a businesswoman with responsibilities. "During the dinner you missed last night, I talked to the hands to get their feelings on the ideas I have for the ranch. A part of me would rather eat dirt than accept help from Wil Abernathy, but you should know he made a very generous offer to lease part of our acreage."

"You talked to the hands about this?"

"Well, they live on the ranch, too. It's their livelihood on the line as much as mine. We can't all run off and be astronauts."

She was ticked. He could see that and he didn't blame her. He had an out and she didn't.

He studied her, and for a long moment all he could see was the way she'd looked in his arms that first night he'd come back here—with the moonlight on her face and her hair, wild and loose, curling around her shoulders and face. He wanted her. He needed to do right by her.

But he wasn't sure how.

"Mick might come back and haunt us both if we make a deal with Abernathy," Ace said slowly. He was well aware of the feud. Even if he thought taking Wil's offer might be a good option, he didn't want to do so at Molly's expense. She was struggling, still grieving her dad and dealing with the will. And he knew she'd feel guilty about letting Abernathy lease the land. Ace needed to be the man Mick had expected him to be, and part of that meant protecting Mick's daughter.

Hell, fake it. Be that man. Solve the problem...
For Molly.

She tipped her head at him. "Glad to see we are on the same page. That means we have to do something more than run cattle. It's just not paying the way it used to. We've still got the oil wells, but they're not producing like they did back in the '70s."

She walked back to the table and pulled out a chair, sitting down as she drew her bag toward her.

He thought about something Dennis had said before Ace had left Houston. About bids for the new training facility and how he wanted the facility to be close by and have more ties to NASA than the civilian team.

What if the Bar T was the location of the facility? It was a long shot. Still, they wouldn't know unless they tried.

He put his hand on hers. "I've got a suggestion, but it's a bit unusual."

"What is it? So far all I've come up with is some sort of B&B spa and no one really wants to do that."

"NASA. I'm part of a team preparing for long-term missions designed as precursors to the Mars missions we hope will happen one day. Much like Project Mercury was preparation for the moon landing. These missions would set up a way station between Earth and

Mars. And they are looking to develop a dedicated training facility."

"How would that work?"

"Well, the facility would be developed and paid for by a company that we agreed to work with. We're close enough to Houston for it to be a good fit. What do you think?" he asked.

MOLLY LOVED HIS IDEA. From what Jason said, it would bring in money for the ranch without too much disruption. The financing would come through the government and private companies. Jason's plan was for her to be a director of the facility along with him. As an experienced astronaut, he'd provide the NASA expertise and with her management skills and some additional training, Molly would be a good candidate for handling many of the day-to-day operational details.

"So you'd be here on the ranch?"

"For now. Once I get cleared for missions it's my intention to go back into training for the Cronus program," he said. "At that point, NASA could hire another qualified person to take on any hands-on responsibilities I would have to give up."

He wasn't going to stay forever because his place was up there, but she could have him for a little while. She was tied to the land. She couldn't imagine living in the stars, but he did. He wanted it.

To agree to this idea of his. "How good do you think our chances are?"

"What?"

"You said *bid*. That means there are other potential places they could use, right?" she asked.

"Yes. I don't know how many, but I can go to Houston and talk to my boss. If Dennis likes the idea, then I will ask him for some contacts with a company that wins a lot of bids."

"Like the Jet Propulsion Laboratory. Right? They built the Mars Rover and do a lot of work for NASA."

"Yes. Like JPL, but smaller. This is a newer program and while everyone is excited about going to Mars one day and doing more long-term exploration, the risks are high. Many companies aren't sure they want to invest in what could be a very short-term project if something goes wrong. But we've got nothing to lose and a good shot at winning the bid. I think my involvement will help. I'm one of only a handful of people who've spent a year in orbit."

She knew he was kind of a big deal with NASA. They'd invested a lot in him and she imagined his knowledge of the training requirements would be a boon. "Okay. I guess we owe it to ourselves to give this a shot, don't we?"

"We do," he said. "How should we word this on the form?"

She looked down at the papers Rupert had given them, tucking a stubborn lock of hair behind her ear as she read. She tried to focus, but she was very aware of Jason standing close. Watching her.

She'd made a decision… She wasn't sure when but there was a surety in her now that hadn't been there before they'd walked into Rupert's office. She was going to take this time with him and not look back. She had thought she'd have her dad with her forever and if his death had shown her anything, it was that she couldn't wait to say and do the things she wanted. Time would keep moving on, of course, and the people who came into her life might move on, too. She had no guarantees of anything with Jason. Even if he never went back to active duty he might leave.

"I'm not sure," she said at last. "You want to read it over? I'll go get Shirley and see if she can help us."

He came closer and she caught a whiff of his aftershave, remembered how she'd breathed it in when they'd laid on the grass and held each other. She closed her eyes and then pushed herself back from the conference room table.

Business. She needed to get this taken care of first, and then put this passion between the two of them to the test. See if it was going to be one quick burst or something that might last longer. There was no denying it. And she was tired of pretending she didn't want him.

She patted him on the ass as she walked by him toward the door.

"Be right back," she said.

But he was quick. She'd had no idea he could move that fast. He reached past her and put his hand on the door. Then he turned her in his arms and leaned over her, his hands on her shoulders as he pressed his body to hers.

"I thought you were mad at me?"

"Don't think. That's been the problem all along. We're young, we want each other and if we know anything it's that life goes fast and we aren't guaranteed anything beyond this moment."

"Really?"

"Hell, yes. I'm tired of being smart and pretending that I don't want you, Jason—I mean, Ace."

"I like that you call me Jason, even though I asked

you to call me Ace. Reminds me that I'm a man, not just an astronaut," he said, putting his forehead against hers.

This time she framed his face with her hands and kissed him. She didn't care about anything except the way his mouth felt against hers. How impossibly right everything about this kiss was to her. She needed. Needed to believe that she was living and not just waiting for something to happen to her.

She was taking what she wanted with both hands.

6

SHE GRABBED HIS WRISTS and pressed his body into the door. Her breasts brushed his chest and he hardened in a rush as she leaned up against him and bit his earlobe.

"What are you doing?"

"Is it really that confusing?" she asked with a wink as she kissed his neck and then bit him lightly. "I'm taking control. I realized that I have been standing still for too long, rocket man."

Rocket man.

His profession meant something to her. He heard the inference in her voice, but he was so turned on by her body close to his that he couldn't figure it out. He couldn't think.

He felt her hair on his neck, soft and smooth, smelling like summer strawberries, and he remembered his long year in orbit and how he'd started craving things. One of them had been sun-warmed strawberries.

He was hard and everything in him was focused on her breasts against his chest, her lips on his skin. The way she held him as if she wasn't going to let go until she had what she wanted from him.

He wanted to give it to her, whatever she needed. Wanted this moment to never end. The air-conditioned coolness of the room contrasted with the heat that was burning inside him. He was inflamed by the way she kissed him, the passion that she'd let slip until it consumed the both of them.

He pulled one his hands free and reached behind her to cup her ass, drawing her forward. The fabric of her dress was light and he imagined he could feel her skin beneath it. He lifted her off her feet as she wrapped one leg around his thigh and pressed against the length of his cock.

Reaching between them, she rubbed her hand over his zipper and his hips jerked toward her touch as her caress moved up his chest and neck. She scraped her fingernail over his jaw and leaned up to whisper in his ear.

"I know that I'm not as mysterious as the universe…"

He let her feet fall to the floor. "The cosmos I can explore and understand through science, but you have always been a mystery to me."

Her lips were red, her skin flushed and desire was still there between them, but he wanted their first time to last the afternoon, not be a hurried coupling in the lawyer's office.

"Let's finish up the paperwork. I want to be alone with you," he said.

She nodded.

She pushed past and walked out the door. He turned to the window that looked out over the street, willing his body to calm down. Reminding himself that he was always in control. But with Molly he wasn't. She rattled him.

Maybe staying at the ranch was stupid, but he'd never been one to back down from a challenge—and this was most definitely a challenge.

He wanted her. Wanted to prove to himself that he could have her and still go off on the adventures that had always defined him. But what about Molly? She'd said she wanted to live for the moment. Did she really understand what that meant? What it would be like when he had to leave?

The door opened behind him and he glanced over his shoulder to see Shirley standing there.

"Molly asked me to show you how to fill in the paperwork," she said.

He nodded and walked around to the other side of the conference table, sitting down across from Rupert's secretary.

"Tell me what you want to use the ranch for," she invited.

He told her, but his mind was on Molly. Where was she? Had she run from him again?

No, she hadn't. She strolled in a few minutes later. He could tell she'd splashed water on her face. She sat down next to Shirley.

He relaxed as soon as she did and he knew that what he'd been telling himself, that making love to Molly would bring him back to normal, had been a lie. There was no way that he was ever going to feel normal where she was concerned. She rattled him on a soul-deep level and made him want things he didn't think he'd ever really be able to have.

Shirley and Molly went to the other room to get more forms and he sat there wondering what was wrong with him. He could see himself living on

Mars or spending his life up amongst the stars, but he couldn't imagine being in a romantic relationship that wasn't fleeting.

When she came back in, he read over the typed notes and the asterisk she'd added at the bottom that said if he was off the planet for more than two years she would be solely responsible for managing their inheritance.

She knew he wasn't staying.

And still she had kissed him like she wasn't going to let him go.

SIGNING THE PAPERS took them into the late afternoon. Rupert wanted them to come back to his office once they knew if the NASA plan would be moving forward. If it didn't work, they'd be back to square one.

Molly listened to Jason telling Rupert about the facility and realized she was out of her depth. She only understood about an eighth of what was said in the meeting. She had a lot of work to do to prepare for this. Though she hoped her main responsibility would simply be liaising with the facility and keeping the ranch and NASA elements separate.

Seeing Jason in his element, listening to the passion in his voice as he spoke about the long-term missions, awed her. When the meeting ended, Rupert stepped out and Jason turned to her, catching her staring.

"You okay?"

She nodded. "This is really different than ranching. I don't know how effective I'll be as a co-director."

He winked at her. "I'll handle the space stuff. You're a great manager," he reminded her.

"I think I'd be better as a liaison," she said, gathering up everything she'd brought with her today and putting it back in her bag."

"Okay, that works, too. Are you expected back for evening chores?" he asked.

"Rina isn't expecting me. I wasn't sure how long this would take."

"Good, would you join me for dinner?"

"That would be nice. What did you have in mind?"

"Ray's Bar-b-que," he said.

Ray's was an institution in Cole's Hill. There were some folks who drove all the way over from Houston or down from San Antonio to eat there. It was a big old smokehouse where they pit-roasted brisket for some of the best barbecue she'd ever had.

"Sounds good. If you go get dinner, I'll pick up some cold beer at the grocery store. We can eat in the park," she said.

"Sounds like a plan. See you there in thirty minutes."

He walked out of the conference room and she sat there for a few more minutes before Shirley came in.

"Are you almost finished?"

"I am."

She left the law offices and walked down to the small grocery store to pick up drinks and dessert. Then she carried the bag back to the park. She sat on the same bench they'd used that morning.

The day hadn't turned out at all as she'd expected. Everything had changed—how she saw Jason, what the future of the ranch might be. She felt panic in her stomach the way she did whenever things changed. Sometimes she felt like the big, worn oak tree that stood behind the barn. Rooted so deeply that the wind barely made the branches sway. She liked it. Consistency was what she wanted and needed. She knew things couldn't stay the same, that change was necessary. But as much as she knew she needed to accept Jason's plan for a new facility in order to keep the ranch in the family and to ensure its continued success, she wasn't too sure about it.

"You're looking way too serious for a picnic," Jason said as he walked up to her. Now he had a baseball cap on, not his usual cowboy hat, and his sunglasses hid his eyes from her.

"Dad used to say I could worry about a new pair of shoes." It wasn't much of an answer, but maybe he'd let it go. *Please*, she thought.

"You always have been very serious. I have a suggestion, if you're game."

"I wouldn't be here if I wasn't," she said.

"Good. I parked next to your truck. Why don't we head back toward the ranch? I know a nice, secluded spot where we can eat our dinner."

That suited her just fine. She needed time alone with her thoughts.

They went back to the trucks, and Molly followed Jason's pickup until he pulled off the road. Then he got out of his truck and hopped in the cab of hers.

"This is our property," she said.

"I know. Drive toward that copse of trees," he said.

She nodded, putting the truck back in gear. They bounced over the field as the sun started sinking low toward the horizon. She parked near the trees. Jason got out and then walked around to the bed of the pickup. He put down the tailgate as she joined him and he climbed into the back of the truck, unfolding a blanket that he must have tossed back there before he'd gotten in the cab.

"You've thought of everything."

"I try. Part of my job is being prepared for anything," he said.

"You must be very good at it."

"I am. That's why I'm determined to make this facility work," he said.

She sat on the tailgate and then swung her legs up, settling down next to Jason on the blanket. She pulled the grocery bag closer and handed him an ice-cold Lone Star beer before taking out a tub of potato salad and some forks. "I didn't get any plates. I figured we could share."

"That works for me," he said, giving her a sandwich.

She opened the paper wrapping and closed her eyes, breathing in the scent of the barbecue beef sandwich. "I swear heaven must smell like this."

He laughed and she blushed. "It's been a while since I've done this."

"I'm sorry I wasn't around when your dad died," he said.

"It's okay. Today in that meeting, I realized you are doing exactly what you should be."

"I've always thought so, but now I'm questioning it," he said, taking a big bite of his sandwich.

She watched him chew before shaking herself and turning away.

"That's just because of your health."

"And you," he said.

She knew he meant the ranch and the attraction, nothing more. And she was fine with that. But a part of her wished it really was about her. Molly, the person, not his business partner, not his fling. Not Mick's daughter.

HE'D NEVER THOUGHT about getting older or the years passing. He always lived his life one day at the time. But he had to face things now. It wasn't just his health that weighed heavily on his mind. Mick had only been sixty-five. He'd probably imagined he had years ahead of him to spend with Molly, get the ranch in order, do everything that mattered. Ace was only thirty-one, but his job was dangerous and life was uncertain. He didn't want to miss out on the important things—and for the first time he wondered if some of those things might be right here on Earth.

"I mean that," he said to Molly. She'd shrugged slightly when he'd said she was part of what was changing him.

"Sure you do. We're partners. We will be taking on a huge responsibility if NASA awards that bid to us," she said. "You better be serious. I have no clue how to do any of it without you."

"You'd figure it out pretty quick. Besides NASA will hire all the other personnel. The Cronus program has a few people in place but they will add more once the facility is built and staffed. Are you happy with this decision?" he asked. "I hope I didn't force it on you."

"I'm okay with it. The only thing that would have truly made me happy was finding a way to go back to how things were. You know?"

"I do know. It's hard to see your home change and to realize that you have to embrace it or lose it."

"It is. I didn't know you thought of the Bar T like that," she said.

He glanced over at her, removing his ball cap and putting his sunglasses inside of it. He took a deep breath.

"I was thinking about my childhood home."

"Oh. What happened there? You never talked about it when we were younger," she said, taking a sip of her beer and shifting on the blanket until she could rest her back against the wheel well, stretching her legs out in front of her. "Unless you don't want to say."

"I wouldn't have brought it up," he said, smiling at her. "I lived in a low-income apartment complex. My old man was gone before I was born. Mom got sick, pancreatic cancer. They moved her to hospice, and after she died no one seemed to remember me. So I just lived in our apartment by myself. The water and electricity worked for about two months and then they shut it off, but no one came to take over the apartment. I started shoplifting food, and then fell in with a bad crowd..."

She reached over and rubbed his leg. "I'm sorry."

"Mick told me everyone knows heartache. Some of us just get more of it than others," Ace said. Mick had been laconic with his words, but what he did say always seemed to be exactly what Ace had needed to hear.

"Sounds like Dad. Being here helped you, didn't it?"

"Yes," he said. "More than I can say."

"When I was younger I never understood why Dad took you boys in. Jeb tried to explain it to me when I was being a bratty teenager and not talking to Dad, but I still didn't get it until just now. We had so much and I'm really glad that Dad invited you and the other boys to share it."

"Me, too," Jason said. Mick had saved him. Not just from jail but also from the man he might have been. Someone who never thought to dream of the stars.

"I am going to have to talk to the bank tomorrow," she said.

He shook his head.

"What?"

"We're on a picnic—no talk of chores or business," he said.

"What will we talk about?"

He leaned against the wheel well on his side and stretched his legs out next to hers. He crossed his arms over his chest. There was so much he wanted to know about her; he wasn't sure where to start.

"What did you do after high school?" he asked.

"Went to community college in Houston for one semester. I got an apartment near campus with Annabelle, do you remember her?"

"Vaguely. You used to hang out with her in the summers, right?" he asked. He had an image of a redheaded girl in his mind, but he wasn't sure if that was Annabelle.

"Yeah. Anyway, turns out she is very messy and not too disciplined, so we didn't like living together and I didn't much like college so I came back home and took some online classes in business management. Dad thought it would be good for me when I took over the ranch."

"Was it?"

"Yes, so far. What did you do when you first left the ranch?" she asked.

He didn't want to talk about himself. He wanted to know more about her. What she'd said about her friend intrigued him. "Are you a clean freak?"

"What?"

"You said Annabelle was messy," he said.

"Oh. I just like things in their place. Orderly, you know. She left stuff everywhere."

"I like things orderly, too," he said.

"That makes sense. On the ISS you have very little room," she said. "What's it like living in such a small space for a year?" she asked. "I think I'd go crazy if I couldn't go outside, breathe in the fresh air and walk through the fields."

She gestured to the ranch and he noticed how slim her arms were, how gracefully she moved.

"You would."

7

"I GUESS YOU have the whole universe spread out before you, though. The ranch must seem small compared to that," she said.

He tipped his head back, staring up. As the sun set and the sky darkened, she saw stars and satellites twinkling in the sky.

"It does. But most of the time all I can do is look at the surrounding stars and the Earth through the space station's windows," he said at last. His voice was low, husky and relaxed. He seemed to be at peace, which she'd never noticed in him before.

"Most of the time?"

"Space walks," he said. "I put on a space suit, tether myself to a line and go out for an extravehicular activity. I love the freedom of floating around up there."

"Isn't that scary?" she asked. She was scared just thinking about him up there, exposed and vulnerable. She reminded herself that he was nothing more than a guy she knew from childhood. A guy who turned her on, made her hotter than a two-dollar pistol as her gramps used to say. Yet he seemed like more than that somehow. He attracted her like nothing—no one— else ever had.

"No more so than galloping across the field when a horse has its head," he said.

"But if you fall from a horse, you don't have far to go."

She was still trying to understand the draw that universe had for him.

"You could easily break your neck and die," he said at last. "But the thrill of letting your horse run across the field, of feeling the wind whipping around you, of being free—it's enough of an incentive that you don't worry about that possibility. You know the risk is worth it."

She uncrossed her legs and sat up from where she'd been leaning. As the darkness deepened and it became harder to see his features, he revealed things he wouldn't say in the light of day. It had been the same two nights ago when he'd gone riding with her.

Why was it they both felt safer in the dark?

She couldn't dwell on that.

"What if your tether breaks? What if you just float away?"

"I'd be out there with the stars, seeing parts of the universe only a handful have ever seen... I'd say that would be worth the cost."

"It seems too big, too scary for me."

"Some of the things you do scare me," he said.

"Like what?" she asked. "You've done everything I do."

He put his hand on her leg, just held it loosely, but a shiver went up her body. "Okay, maybe that's true, but I hated it—at least when I first arrived at fourteen. I was so dusty and dirty and every night when I went to bed, I'd stare out the window above my bed and think about being up there with the stars."

Even when he'd been closest to her, he'd been just out of her reach. She knew this. Why did she keep trying to find some way to convince herself he was the kind of man who'd stay?

She should stop thinking of him as Jason and remember he was Ace. That's all he could ever be to her.

Ace.

Superstar astronaut. Heart in the stars. He was here because he was grounded. As soon as the all clear came he'd be gone.

He hadn't even hesitated to sign that document earlier that had given her the right to make all decisions about the ranch if he was off the planet for more than two years.

"Why did Dad give you half the ranch?" she asked.

He shrugged. But she felt that he knew more.

"Don't lie."

"Lifting my shoulders isn't lying," he said.

"Not telling the truth is. Please, tell me," she said.

"He told me once that he was afraid you'd never have a chance to be anything more than what he and the Bar T had made you. I guess he didn't want to put the full weight of owning the ranch on you. Maybe he thought I'd be able to help."

She could hear her father's voice in Jason's words. Heard the worry he'd felt in the last few months before his accident. Tears burned her eyes and she blinked, trying to stem them, but failed. "Why didn't he ask me what I wanted?"

"Maybe he was afraid of the answer."

She hugged herself and put her head down. The ache she felt for her father was all-consuming. She just wanted one more hug. One more chance to smell that unique scent of Old Spice aftershave and worn leather. To know she didn't have to worry because he was there.

She felt Jason's hand on her arm.

"I'm sorry," he said.

"Me, too. I… What did he think I'd do?"

"Live. He said that he suspected you were hiding from something here," Jason said.

She went still. The tears stopped and she realized her father knew there was more to her coming back from Houston than a messy roommate.

"What are you hiding from?"

TALKING NEVER WAS her strong suit. She'd never learned to hide what she was feeling, to protect herself. She pulled her arm out from under Jason's and scooted toward the end of the truck. She hopped down and stood there. Twilight had darkened and she was caught between night and day. She was dressed up rather than wearing her usual jeans and scuffed boots. She almost felt like she didn't belong here right now.

She was a mess. She'd been pretending for too long that she wasn't. Thought she was going to make a deal with Jason and somehow get the ranch back on solid financial ground once and for all. But now she acknowledged she'd been kidding herself. She was never going to get out of this morass.

She knew it as surely as she knew that she'd been sending mixed signals all day. She wanted him. She wanted to lose herself in that sweet crush she remembered from a more innocent time. When she'd had no idea what real heartbreak and loss felt like.

Jason slid to the end of the pickup truck and sat there, his legs hanging over the tailgate as he quietly watched her. She noticed that he had on some kind of hiking boot, not Western boots. He wasn't a cowboy. How many times was she going to have to be faced with that knowledge before it sank in?

"You okay?"

No.

"Of course. I mean, you just told me my dad thought I was hiding, and I had to make a deal that requires me to let strangers come onto my land. I'm partners with a man I barely know…yeah, I'm great."

"Sarcasm doesn't suit you," he said.

"Sorry. It's all I've got right now. It's that or howling," she admitted. "Since I want to preserve a little dignity I'm going with sarcasm."

"You can howl with me," he said.

"Don't."

"Don't what?"

"Be nice. Be agreeable. I don't want—"

She broke off and turned away.

"You need a fight," he said.

She didn't answer him. Now she felt stupid. And small and silly. And still so freaking lost. She knew this made no sense. But then, emotions weren't logical. She'd learned that a long time ago.

"Yeah, but that's not fair to you."

"Since when has life been fair?" he asked.

"Never," she said under her breath. Her mom had died, his dad had left, his mom had died, her lover had left, her dad had died and who the hell knew what else had happened to Jason.

"Damned straight," he said, hopping off the tailgate and putting his hands on her shoulders.

She turned to face him.

"Remember when you pinned me against the door in Rupert's office?" he asked.

"How could I forget that?"

"I've been waiting for us to be alone all afternoon so we could finish what we started. I want that passion, Mol. I want you."

"I want you, too. I'm trying to justify sleeping with you, trying to remember that nothing lasts and that I can just do this," she said.

She put her hand on his chest. Felt his body heat through the fabric and watched him, carefully. It wasn't light enough to see his eyes, but she felt his gaze on her.

"We'll always be friends," he said.

And that should be enough. She wasn't going to fall in love. She remembered the one time she had fallen for a man. How much it had hurt when it ended. Could she keep her emotions bottled up?

Hell, probably not, but damned if she was going to deny herself Jason.

"Yes, we will," she said at last.

She wrapped her arms around him, intending to kiss him, but instead she put her head on his chest. For just a moment she needed to feel him wrapped around her. She needed to know this was more than just physical because her emotions were still chaotic, swirling through her like a tornado across the plains.

And she needed to be sure that he was solid enough to take the buffeting from the wind.

He rubbed his hands over her back, his fingers massaging her sides all the way down to her butt and then back up. Those long, languid caresses brought her more fully into her body and she felt the tension and worry drift away.

There was only the two of them and this moment. Nothing lasted forever.

But she wanted this time with Jason to be lived to the fullest. Not hiding or running or worrying.

Tomorrow she might struggle with that, but for tonight…she was his.

And he was hers.

She lifted her face to his and he lowered his head, his mouth falling on hers with all the pent-up desire she felt sweeping through her own body. With all the lust and need they had awakened in the lawyer's office. She'd thought she'd pushed it aside but realized the fires had only been banked, not extinguished.

His tongue pushed deep into her mouth as his hands grabbed her ass and lifted her off her feet.

She wrapped her legs around his lean waist and held on to his shoulders as the night swirled around her and she heard a moan. It was deep, raw and needy.

JASON SLIPPED HIS hands up the back of her thighs, clutching them to hold her up but also because he loved the feel of her flesh under his hands. Her skin was supple and smelled sweet. Under the perfume was another musk that was all Molly. Seductive and sensual, it aroused him as much as touching her thighs did.

He fanned his fingers out wider to reach her inner

thighs and to feel the heat of her sex on his skin. She was so hot. And so damned soft. Softer than anything else he'd ever touched. He held her, his tongue in her mouth, his cock hard against the apex of her thighs, and took everything she had to give.

She was lost. He'd felt the loneliness that had come off her in waves. He'd experienced the same thing himself as a teen. That need had awakened in him a keen longing to give her something of himself. To make promises he knew he could never keep no matter how much he wanted to. To show her that she wasn't alone. That they could lose themselves in each other and forget everything else for a few bliss-filled hours with only the stars and moon looking on.

He tore his mouth from hers, his breath sawing in and out. She bit his lower lip gently and then licked her own. He groaned and stopped thinking about anything but his thickening erection and how much he wanted her.

He took two steps back until he felt the cold metal of the pickup truck behind him. The gate dug into his back as Molly undulated against him. He felt her long, cool fingers on his neck; she stroked his pulse, which he knew raced.

He shifted her weight to one arm and saw her tight nipples pressing against the fabric of her sundress. Unable to help himself, he leaned down to suck on one of them through her clothing. She arched her back, thrusting her breasts toward him. He palmed her other breast as he continued to suck on her nipple.

He felt the strain a little in his muscles, but he'd been working out every day for most of his adult life and if he couldn't hold on to this wild cowgirl while he was making love to her, then what was the point? She moaned his name and he felt her hands in his hair, tracing the shape of his ear before moving down his neck again.

She stroked his chest and then wedged her hand between their bodies to run her fingers down the line of his zipper. His hips jerked forward and he had to shift his hold on her as a wave of need, hot like a solar flare, washed over him.

There was no hiding his reaction to her. And he didn't want to. For the first time since he'd come back to Cole's Hill and the Bar T Ranch, he felt like he was being true to himself. Every breath he took was filled with the scent of her. The feel of her under his fingers inflamed every sense in his body. He was compelled by the need to fill her completely.

He turned to set her ass on the tailgate and stand between her legs as he tangled his hands in the hair at the nape of her neck, tugging lightly on it. She let her head fall back, exposing the long length of her neck. He kissed it, moving his mouth slowly down to her collarbone where the fabric of her sundress blocked his access to her skin.

She wrapped her arms around his shoulders and tightened her legs around his hips, then shoved the strap of her dress down. He groaned in approval and kissed his way farther down her arm. Moving slowly back toward her torso, he followed the neckline of her dress, dipping his tongue underneath to taste more of her.

She was addictive. He wanted to see her stretched out under him. Naked so that he could explore her entire body. Wanted nothing but his hands and mouth on her. Wanted her to need him and nothing else.

He pushed her legs farther apart, caressing her knees and slowly moving his hands down her legs to her feet. He took off her left boot and set it on the ground before turning his attention to the right. He removed it as well and then pulled off her socks.

He smiled when he saw they were decorated with pink flamingoes. He set them on the truck bed. Lifting her left foot, he placed it in the center of his chest. She wriggled her toes and he rubbed the arch of her foot.

"Your feet are small."

"Really? They seem just right to me."

He ran his finger along her instep, tickling her, and she squirmed to get away, causing the hem of her dress to ride up her thighs. All thoughts of smallish feet and tickling her dropped away. He noticed the large bruise on the top of her foot and pressed a gentle kiss to it. Ranching was hard work. He'd ask her what happened later, make sure it wasn't causing her pain. But right now he wanted to focus on bringing them both pleasure. His fingers glided up her leg. It was strong, muscled from years of working on the ranch—he always associated Molly with strength.

Despite what her father had said, and what she was going through now, he didn't believe she was hiding on the Bar T—that wasn't Molly Tanner's way. She was the kind of woman who met life head-on and took what she wanted. And for some reason she wanted him.

He hoped he wouldn't disappoint her. But at this moment, with the scent of her filling every breath he took, the only thing he could be sure of was how much he wanted her.

He just needed to be inside of her. To prove to himself that he wasn't lost.

Damn.

He shut down his mind and just stared at her long, slim legs. Her skirt still covered the top of her thighs and suddenly the clothing wasn't tolerable to him anymore.

"You're so beautiful," he said, the words torn from some place deep in his soul.

"I'm not," she argued.

"You are." His fingers drifted higher and felt something rough on her inner thigh. Somehow he hadn't noticed it earlier. Leaning lower, he examined her leg in the dusky twilight.

"What is this?" he asked.

"Burn scar from the time Annabelle and I tried smoking in the barn, but Jeb busted us. I dropped the cigarette in surprise but caught it between my legs, not wanting to start a fire in the hay. It burned my jeans instead."

He touched the scar again, lightly. The skin was raised, but it wasn't as rough as it would have been when she'd first got it.

"When was this?"

"The spring before you arrived."

"You tried smoking at twelve?" he asked. No matter how much he learned about her, there was still a lot he didn't know.

"Yeah, my mom had just died. I was going through a phase," she said.

He feathered his fingers over the patch of skin. It fit with what he knew of Molly.

He leaned down and kissed the scar.

What else had she done? What other scars were hidden on her body? He vowed to find them all. To search them out so he could kiss them and soothe them. To make her his completely and learn all the secrets that he'd never realized she was keeping.

But how could he do that and still keep his own secrets? It was a path he'd have to tread very carefully.

He kept kissing her, moving higher and higher until he reached the edge of her panties. He mouthed her through her underwear and felt the heat of her body. Her thighs tightened around his head and then she let them fall open.

He pushed her panties to one side and parted her with his fingers. Her hair was neatly trimmed, her flesh a delicate pink and the little nub at the center was swollen with need. He gently caressed her, rubbing her clit in a circular motion, and she moaned. A sound of approval. He continued to move his finger over her before he leaned down closer again.

He breathed on her first, watching her legs spread wider apart as she lifted her hips, presenting her body to him. He ran his tongue over her and she grabbed his head, resting one of her legs on his shoulder as he continued to lick her delicate flesh. She tasted amazing. He traced her core with his finger, just teasing the opening, and then slowly pushed one finger up inside of her. Her hips jerked upright.

He added a second finger and thrust them deeper. She was the perfect dessert on this starry night. She felt like everything to him in this moment. He was rock hard, his cock straining against the zipper of his jeans, but he didn't want to stop touching Molly to free it. He continued moving his mouth over her until he felt her body start to tighten around his fingers. He kept rocking them in and out of her until she arched her back and cried his name.

He lifted his head, pulled his fingers from her body and looked up at her. She was on her elbows gazing down at him. Her eyes were fiery, passionate. There was a flush to her body and her breath rasped in and out, causing her breasts to rise and fall rapidly.

"That was…"

"Delicious."

He climbed up on the tailgate and straddled her as she reached for the zipper of his jeans. He had a condom. Just one. Optimistically put in his pocket earlier when he'd stopped for gas on the way to the coffee shop.

He'd wanted her for so long. He'd known it when he arrived on the Bar T, and that deep need for her had been confirmed today in the lawyer's office when he'd realized he wanted to be her hero. He wanted to come up with a solution that not only would be palatable to her but would impress her.

Shit. He was thirty-one and still trying to figure out how to impress a girl he liked. He'd hoped maybe he'd have figured women out by this age. Now he was wise enough to know he never would.

But he knew what she wanted tonight and he meant to give it to her. Some things in his life were out of his control right now, but with Molly there were no limits. He was in charge and he meant to take full advantage of that tonight.

She reached into the opening of his jeans as she lowered the zipper; he felt her hand rubbing up and down his cock. He jerked forward and realized his control was more tenuous than he'd imagined.

He had been at the space station for a year and that was a long time without anything besides his fantasies to keep him company. His body was primed. And this was Molly…which made it so much sweeter.

She traced his length, her fingernail scraping over his boxers. He wanted to feel her touch on his naked skin. He quickly freed himself, the evening air brushing over his aroused flesh, as she scooted backward, coming up on her knees to look at him.

She took his shaft in one hand, stroking him in her fist. Moving it up and down in a slow and sensuous way that made his balls tighten. She skimmed her finger over the tip of his erection and his hips jerked forward.

She cupped him in one hand and squeezed very softly as she tightened her grip on his cock. He started to thrust in her hand. She leaned forward and he felt her breath on him a moment before her tongue traced the head of his penis.

The beginning of his orgasm shivered up and down his spine and he pressed his hips forward, feeling her mouth engulf him. He tried to control himself—he'd been lauded for his self-control. But her mouth made a mockery of that. He was thrusting into her mouth, his hands in her hair and her hands on his balls.

But he wanted more for this first encounter with her. He forced himself to pull back. She followed him. But he tipped her chin up and looked down into her eyes.

"I need to be inside of you," he said.

She nodded. "I want that, too."

She reached under her dress and removed her panties. Then she looked at him. He put the condom on with one hand and then drew her closer until she straddled his lap. His hands under her dress, he felt the warmth of her body in contrast to the cool fabric.

He ran his hands down her spine; she arched over him and brought her mouth down hard on his. She took one of his hands and brought it to her breast. He cupped it and then pushed the fabric out of his way.

She reached behind her, pulled the dress over her head and tossed it away. Then, she slowly undid the buttons on the front of his shirt. She pushed it aside and leaned down to kiss him. One of his hands tangled in her hair as their mouths met again and he shifted his hips so that the tip of his cock was poised at the entrance of her body.

She hovered over him and then slowly lowered herself down his length. He sucked her tongue deeper into his mouth. She stopped, letting her body adjust to his size, and then she rocked up until he was almost completely out of her before plunging back down on him.

She tore her mouth from his, tipping her head back as she rode him hard. He pushed the fabric of her bra out of his way and found her nipple with his mouth. He sucked on her and felt her moving faster and more forcefully against him. But it wasn't enough. He needed more.

He grabbed her hips, clutching at her ass, as he drove himself up into her and pulled her down against him. The fire of sex engulfed them both as they drove themselves harder and harder until she screamed his name and he felt her tightening around him. He held her hips tight against him as he continued to thrust up into her, sucking her nipple deeper into his mouth until he felt his balls tighten and he came. Emptying himself, he continued to thrust into her until he was spent.

She collapsed against him, her head on his shoulder. He held her loosely, but he wanted to clutch her to him. Wanted to remember this moment, her pressed against him like a warm blanket, when he was back in the coldness of space.

"Well, you showed me the stars tonight," she said, her voice breathless and her tone, he suspected, deliberately light.

"And you showed me how little I know of the universe. That there are still so many mysteries I have yet to understand."

He drew her dress over her and held her in his arms. He wanted to pretend that this had changed nothing, but instead it seemed that everything was different now. He held her so close that it was impossible to deny it.

She'd become important to him.

She'd made a place inside his soul.

8

JASON TOLD HER about the night sky as he held her in his arms. In the distance there was nothing but endless inky darkness. They were too far from town to see the flickering streetlights and too far from the buildings on the ranch to see their lights, either. It was as if they were the only two people on the planet at this moment.

"Is that the appeal of traveling to Mars or another far-off planet?" she asked. "Being the only person there…well, apart from the rest of the crew, of course."

"Some of it," he said. "Part of it is that when I'm up there I don't have the worries I do on Earth. I just have to do my job. And everything is mission critical. I can't stop to worry about anything else."

"I wouldn't mind getting away from my worries here," she said. "But I'd miss the ranch."

He tightened his arms around her and smoothed her hair absently. He was mellow. Hell, she was, too. It was as if sex had reset something inside of her that she hadn't realized was askew.

"What would you run away from?" he asked.

She thought about it for a moment. She could tell

him anything. That was what it felt like tonight. He was warm and comforting as he held her.

"Just all the doubts that I have," she said. "I get so tired of wondering if I'm doing what Dad wanted. I hate that he's not here. I wish… I almost wish he'd been sick for a little while so I could have had some warning, been able to say good-bye, but that's selfish. He would have hated being stuck in bed, unable to take care of things around the ranch. Still, it would have been easier for me."

He rubbed her arm up and down.

"I wish I'd been here. As much as I like being up there…I wish I'd been here for you when Mick had his accident. I wish I'd told him at least once how grateful I am for what he did for me," Jason said.

She squeezed his wrist. "He knew."

"Really?"

"Yes. He was very proud of you. He told everyone who came to the ranch, didn't matter if they were delivering feed or a new stud. Dad would tell them about his 'son' the astronaut."

Jason squeezed her tight and she heard his breath catch. She turned to look at him, but he'd tipped his head up toward the sky and she gave him a moment. Gave him the time he needed to get his emotions under control.

That was the thing about grief, she thought—it wasn't just over and done. It kept sweeping along and hitting her when she least expected it. But talking about Dad tonight felt right. Felt like they both needed to get some sort of closure in regard to the man who'd meant the world to both of them and had left them so unexpectedly.

She knew that if it hadn't been for Mick's death, she and Jason wouldn't be here. They would both be living their ordinary lives.

"I miss him," she said.

"I know. What do you think he'd say about us turning part of the ranch into a training facility?"

"I have no idea," she said. "It's different. Is this your way of staying with NASA even if you don't pass the medical?"

He shrugged. She noticed he did that a lot when he didn't want to answer a question. She got it. It was easier for her to talk about him than to examine herself.

"Sort of," he said. "Ever feel like you were born at the wrong time?"

"Not really. I'm pretty happy right where I am."

"Yeah, I can see that. That's probably why everything has hit you so hard with your dad," he said. "I mean…"

She reached up and touched his face. "I get it. Why do you wish you were born in a different time?"

"Well, if I was born thirty years earlier, I could have been part of the moon landing and those missions. Twenty years later and I'd be the perfect age to land on Mars one day. Instead…"

"You are doing the work to enable others to go to Mars. To allow us to see if there is other life in the universe," she said. "This facility—the missions you would be training astronauts for are key to the next step."

He squeezed her tighter. "I sound like a punk, complaining like that."

"I wouldn't word it like that," she said.

"No, you're much too nice. But my buddies in the Cronus program…"

"Like who? Tell me about them. Are there any women?" she asked. "I'm friends with Jessie Odell, the adventurer, and she does some crazy-ass stuff—surviving in the wilderness, going places where very few men and even fewer women have been."

"I've heard of her. Who hasn't?" Jason said. "How do you know her?"

"We're pen pals. After my smoking incident in the barn, Dad thought I needed a better use of my time. So he found her fan mail address—she was still doing that show with her parents—and I wrote to her. I told her about living on the ranch. She grew up on the ocean and…we connected. We both were isolated in our own ways."

"That's pretty cool. I felt that way when I got assigned to my first mission and started training with Dennis. He'd done a bunch of missions, but we connected. He's like a big brother to me."

"And now he's the guy in charge of the Cronus program, right?"

"Yes. If I pass my medical tests, I'll be competing for a place in his program, along with a bunch of other guys."

"Do you know most of them?" she asked.

"Yeah. I'm probably one of the senior astronauts."

"You're not that old," she said.

"Geez, thanks," he said. "I meant because of the mission-hours I've clocked."

"I know it will be very hard for you if you're grounded permanently," she said. "Why would you want the facility here, outside Houston? Won't that make it even worse?"

"I've spent my entire career working toward manned missions to Mars and making sure we will be prepared to form a colony there one day. I need to know what's out there. But if I'm grounded, I at least want to be involved in some way. I'd never be able to leave NASA completely."

In his voice she heard the same pain and longing she felt when she thought about losing the ranch. He would help her save the Bar T—she knew even if they didn't win the bid, Jason wouldn't leave until the ranch was secure. And now she wanted to do as much for him. She would help him get into shape, do whatever he needed to be ready for his medical. Not for herself, because she was just realizing how much she'd miss him, but for him.

WELL, GETTING DRESSED wasn't awkward at all. Molly handed him his clothes and then he followed her back to the ranch. Rina wasn't in the kitchen, but she'd left half a blueberry pie in the middle of the table with a Post-it note that said there was homemade ice cream in the fridge.

Molly raised her eyebrows at him. "Do you want pie?"

"Yeah, and maybe some decaf," he said. "But I need a shower."

She tipped her head to the side, watching him with a guarded look. "I think you are all right."

She was probably right, but now that he was back in this house he felt the walls closing in on him. He needed to get away for a few minutes. Needed time to think.

Molly was great, but she made him want things that weren't in his plans. She made the ranch feel like... well, hell, it felt like home. And he didn't want that. The Bar T Ranch was his temporary stopover, nothing more.

"Yeah, but I'd still like a shower. Meet me back down here in thirty?" he asked.

She shook her head. "I'm going to skip dessert and head up. I have to be up early to do chores with the men. I've missed them two days in a row. Jeb will give me hell if I'm not there tomorrow."

"Okay," he said.

The distance between them was creeping back in. Though he'd thought he wanted that, he realized he didn't want it this way. He didn't want to feel like he'd done or said the wrong thing. But he was pretty sure he had.

When hadn't he said the wrong thing? "I'm sorry. It's just...tonight was..."

"Don't say anything else. I'm tired. Like I said, I've got to be up early and tonight was nice. I wish it didn't have to end, but it's like those old stories about the man in the moon. When we look at it too long it falls apart. Let's say good-night now before I make this awkward."

But it was too late. He knew it and he read in her eyes that she did, too. He wanted to apologize again, but she must know he hadn't meant for this to happen. Didn't she? "Do you need me in the morning?"

"Nah. You might want to ride some of the fences tomorrow and get the lay of the land again. You can take out the Mule, the all-terrain vehicle. I'll assign one of our hands to take you around."

"Okay. I also want to see the acreage you spoke of using for the facility."

"Jeb is working on clearing it. We haven't used it for cattle in a while. We can talk it over at breakfast if you're up that early or at lunch, which is at noon."

"I'll be at breakfast," he said.

She nodded. "Night."

She walked out of the room and he just watched her leave. He sat down hard at the table and looked around the big ranch kitchen. The hardwood table that had been built to serve the ranch hands. It was sturdy, well used. Like he felt tonight. Not on its last leg, but worn and scarred. He wanted to believe that he was managing life and all that it threw at him, but tonight he wasn't.

He wanted… Hell, he had no idea. Sex was supposed to be a stress relief. Wasn't that what Hemi always called it? But sex with Molly wasn't just physical. It was more like finding another part of his soul—a part he'd never even knew existed—and feeling as if he was a little closer to being whole.

A person couldn't be that for him. He didn't trust the universe to keep the people he cared about alive and with him. He kept his relationships carefully limited. Mick, Dennis, maybe Hemi and a few of the other guys who were trying for the Cronus missions. That was it. He didn't let many people get close to him and he had the uncomfortable feeling that Molly had slipped in when he hadn't been paying attention.

Her long legs and curvy hips had distracted him.

Made him think with his dick instead of his brain. And now he was dealing with the fallout.

He put his head in his hands, stared at the tabletop and saw a small crescent moon etched into the wood. Dropping his hands, he traced the old carving. He remembered how rebellious he'd felt when he'd worked on it over the course of his first summer at the ranch. He'd felt like he had a secret. Tonight he'd unconsciously sat in the same spot that had been his all those years ago. He glanced across the table, remembered that Molly had sat there.

It was funny that no matter how much had changed this still felt like his spot. He rubbed the moon again. He had always been so sure of what he wanted, where he wanted to go, where his real home was—up there in the stars—but as he looked around the kitchen and the memories of the past swelled around him, he realized he had more of a home here than he wanted to remember.

HE LEFT BEFORE dawn broke over the horizon the next day. Making love to Molly…well, that hadn't been his smartest idea, but he didn't regret it.

As much as ranching wasn't in his plans, he owed it to Mick to make sure that the place survived.

Despite his desire to ride the fences and see the acreage they'd discussed the night before, he didn't want to wait another moment before putting their plan into action. That was why he'd left. It wasn't cowardice driving him from her arms; it was determination. Or at least that was his story and he was sticking to it. He fiddled with the radio and had a flashback to this first ride out to the Bar T Ranch sitting in the front seat with Mick.

The older man had been larger than life and his voice the kind of quiet rumble that rolled through a room the way thunder did across the wide-open plains. He'd hit the different buttons on the radio and looked over at Jason—he'd definitely only been Jason back then—and said, "You like this kind of music?"

Jason hadn't said anything. Still mad that he'd gotten busted for living alone and scared that legally he had to live with this guy.

Finally, after exhausting all of the choices, Mick turned to him, stared with those wise eyes of his and said, "You don't like much, do you?"

Jason had shrugged. He'd been living alone for six months after his mom died. For most of that time there had been no electricity, no music. "I don't know."

"Fair enough," Mick said. "Now that you're living with us, you can figure it out."

Mick had turned on a country music station. Not one of the modern ones. One that played classic country like George Jones, Hank Williams, Jr. and Conway Twitty. And Jason had been hooked. Mick knew it and kept him supplied with CDs and a new CD player in his room. It was the first thing he'd liked about his new life. That, and the fact that he didn't have to worry about finding his next meal or keeping warm at night.

Now, he stopped on that old classic country station. "Who's Gonna Fill Their Shoes?" by George Jones began to play, and tears burned the back of Ace's eyes. He wondered if there'd ever be a man who could fill Mick's shoes. Ace was determined to do right by Molly and the ranch. It was the least he could do for the man who'd saved his life and made this future possible.

And there was Molly. He wanted her to always have the land she loved. To always be able to get on her horse and take that midnight ride across the pasture. He didn't want them to have to sell or lease a single acre.

He had texted Dennis as soon as he had a decent signal and told him he was coming to the base today. He got a response thirty minutes later confirming the appointment.

He thought he should probably contact Molly, but what would he say?

Last night, much like the day he'd first come to the Bar T Ranch, had shown him a glimpse of another life. He was tempted by it, by her, but his heart belonged to NASA, to exploring new worlds, discovering new places.

But he *was* tempted. For the first time since…well, since he'd first kissed her all those years ago.

As he drove on base at Johnson Space Center he still had that feeling of excitement he'd had the first time he'd set foot on the property. Being an astronaut had never become old hat to him—there was nothing routine about his life or about what he did for a living.

He was early for his appointment so he headed over to astronaut quarters. His apartment was in the Mercury building. He walked up the drive just as Hemi "Thor" Barrett was exiting.

"Ace, man, glad to see you. That was a short medical leave." Hemi gave Ace a bro hug and stepped back. Hemi had been his right-hand man on many missions. Since the station was international they were often up there with astronauts from other countries and it was always nice to talk to someone from home. Hemi had on a pair of aviator-style sunglasses and his standard NASA-issued sweats.

"It's not over, unfortunately, and I'm not here for long. But the situation is complicated and I don't want to keep you," Ace replied.

"You aren't keeping me from anything except a five-mile run and I can do that any time before eight when I have a hot date. Is it coffee- or beer-complicated?"

"Beer, but it's too early for that. Plus I've got a meeting with Dennis in thirty."

"Walk and talk?" Hemi asked.

"Yeah…"

"So, besides exercising, what are you doing with your time?"

"Well, remember that ranch I grew up on?"

"Yeah, anyone who's had to listen to your Conway Twitty CDs remembers it."

Ace punched Hemi in the arm. "Watch it."

"What's up with the ranch?"

"I inherited half of it and I'm going to be there for a while straightening things out. Do you know much about the new Cronus training facility they're talking about building?"

"Nah, just that they are looking to outsource it. Dennis isn't happy about some of the bidders. He told us a few days ago that he didn't like working with civilians. Why?"

Ace bit back a smile. That sounded just like Dennis. He liked everything military so no one questioned his orders. They'd reached the base headquarters and he and Hemi stopped in front of the program manager's office.

"Drinks later? I want to hear what you're up to. Or are you heading out after your appointment?" Hemi asked.

"I can do lunch," Ace said.

"See you then."

9

DESPITE HER DETERMINATION to join the hands for chores, Molly woke up late. Well, late for her. Her sleep had been plagued with haunting images of her ancestors frowning at her as she let the Abernathy family lease their land. She'd have no choice but to accept Wil's offer if the bid for the training facility wasn't successful.

She needed to do something to move their plan forward. She showered and got dressed and then looked at herself in the mirror and decided to leave her hair down today. She went downstairs to find Rina singing along to Beyoncé and cutting up meat to go in the slow cooker.

"Late night?" Rina asked as Molly went for the coffeepot.

"Yeah. Still not sleeping well," Molly said. Last night had been different. She didn't want to dwell on it as she knew Jason wasn't long for Cole's Hill and the Bar T Ranch. He'd be back up on missions as soon as he could make it happen, no matter what they decided to do with the ranch.

"Have you seen, Jason—I mean Ace—this morning?" she asked Rina.

Rina chuckled. "Yeah, that boy lit out of here early."

"Oh? Did he say where he was going?" Molly asked.

"Nope. He wasn't too sure he'd be back for dinner," Rina said.

Figures.

He was gone already.

Molly took her coffee down the hall to the office to work on the books. Their finances looked just as bleak as the last time she'd gone over them. They needed a solution. Something that would bring an influx of cash to keep the ranch going. How long would the NASA bidding process take? Could she count on Jason to see it through? Was there anything she could do now to hurry it along?

Molly just knew if she leased the acres to Wil she was going to bring down a shitload of bad karma on herself. But she had to consider all her—*their*—options at this point.

She found the hair elastic that she kept in her pocket and pulled her hair up into a ponytail.

Rina brought in a tray with lunch and some sweet iced tea on it and placed it on the desk before plopping down in the guest chair. The chair was a dusty old recliner that her mom had told her dad to throw out years ago, but Mick had never been able to part with it.

"You've been in here a long time," Rina said. "What's up?"

"Just trying to decide how much bad karma I can handle if I make a deal with Wil Abernathy for part of the land."

"That bad?"

"Worse. Remember that spa we went to up near New Braunfels last year?" she asked Rina. Sometimes she and the housekeeper, who was really more like a friend, would decide they'd had enough of all the testosterone on the ranch and declare it "girls' weekend."

"Yeah, why?"

"Do you think people would pay to come out here and stay?" Molly asked. It was the only other idea she had that didn't involve leasing part of the land.

"Maybe. We have the river and the pond is nice. Plus we could have trail riding out to the pond. Mick had talked about fixing the dock. The pond is already stocked so you could offer fishing," Rina said.

Rina had some really good ideas and Molly jotted them down beside the ones she already had. Of course, she'd have to run them by her partner...if he came back. Jason seemed enthusiastic about the NASA bid, but there was more at stake for her and she had to keep an open mind.

"What's the matter, sunshine? You look sad," Rina asked.

"Just miss Dad," she said.

"I do, too. I never thought I'd miss that cantankerous old coot, but I do. I wasn't ready for our fights to end."

Rina and her dad had fought like brother and sister. There was love under it, but they'd still both been stubborn and very sure they were always right. Rina was ten years younger than her dad. She was more of a surrogate aunt than a mom to Molly.

"Me, neither. I could use his stubbornness now, I think."

Molly glanced down at the list and doodled Jason's

name on the top of it. "What am I going to do with him?"

"Nothing," Rina said, following Molly's train of thought. "Just do you. He'll take care of himself. Isn't he going back to NASA and on another mission soon?"

She drew a scroll pattern down the side of the paper. Doodled the words *To boldly go* underneath it, remembering Jason's tattoo. His health was his business to discuss and so she just shrugged at Rina, but she was concerned. If his condition improved, would he still want to pursue his training-facility idea? It was clear he didn't want to work on the ranch. Originally, he had wanted her to buy him out.

She added that to her list.

"I don't want to have to mortgage any of the land. That was what Dad was trying to avoid when he borrowed money from Jason."

"You can only play the cards you're dealt. Your dad knew it and you do, too. Don't try to do right by him. He's gone and he wanted you to be happy. Do right by you, Molly. Does one option sound better to you than the others?"

"No. I don't want people on our land. I want it to remain the way it always was...but I also wish Dad were here riding out checking fences and doing his chores."

Rina stood up and came around the desk, leaning over to hug her, and Molly just turned her head to the side and hugged Rina back. Tears burned the back of her eyes and she felt more lost now than she ever had in her life. But there wasn't another person who could make this decision for her. And as supportive as Rina was, she was an employee of the ranch like the hands.

Molly knew she couldn't screw this up. She brushed her hand over her eyes and shifted back.

"Thanks, Rina."

"No problem, sunshine. You will figure this out. You always do."

DENNIS LOCK HAD been an astronaut on the shuttle missions and had been Ace's mentor since he was recruited by NASA. Ace trusted the older man and respected him. The news about Ace's slow recovery hadn't been easy for either of them. But it was all part of Dr. Tomlin's research.

"You're back pretty quick," Dennis said. "I doubt your bone density has improved much in the last few days."

Ace nodded as he shook his hand and then took a seat in one of the guest chairs.

"I'd be just as shocked as you if it had. I'm here for another reason. I have recently inherited half of a 760-acre ranch about an hour's drive from here and we need to figure out what to do with the land. They only use about a third of it. I want to know more about the new Cronus facility. Has the bidding for that project closed yet?"

Dennis leaned back in his chair, crossing his arms over his chest. He was in his early fifties and wore his salt-and-pepper hair in a military style. The former astronaut had been married and divorced three times while he'd still been active.

"Not yet. But it's getting close," Dennis said, pulling his keyboard toward him. "Are you thinking you want to bid on it?"

"Yes. It would be a solution to both of our problems," Ace said. Molly and the Bar T would be secure and it was one way he'd be able to continue working with NASA no matter the outcome of his bone-density test in three months' time.

"You won't be able to pull together a winning bid on your own. You'll need assistance from a defense subcontractor."

"Do you know anyone?" Ace asked. "Or do you think this idea is bat-shit crazy?"

"I like it. You know I don't want some yahoo who thinks it would be cool to be a part of NASA to get the bid. Or some billionaire who has always wanted to be the first person to own property on the moon."

"Isn't there a screening process designed to weed those out?" Ace asked. He heard the rancor in Dennis' tone and knew the older man thought of these projects as almost sacred. Something that should only be pursued by men and women who are driven more by a love of exploration than a desire for commercial success.

"Sure. But there are some civilians with too much money who've never heard the word *no*. I like this idea, Ace. So Molly would be the liaison between the ranch and the facility and you'd…well, if you're not on the missions, you could be part of the training staff. How long are you in Houston?"

"As long as I need to be," he said. God, he hoped he was on one of the missions.

"Let me make a few calls to some old contracting friends. I'll see if any are interested in partnering with you. Most of the qualified companies bidding have worked with us before and I know that your land is a prime location for this project. Is it just you? Are you able to make this decision on your own?"

"It's not just me, but my partner has agreed to it," Ace said.

"Good. That's all I need for now."

"I'm going to be on base for a little while. Text me if you hear anything."

"I will. We need to get moving on this for you to have any chance in hell of getting your bid in on time. You're cutting it close," Dennis said. You'll need to work with an experienced defense subcontractor. Everyone submits their bids on the deadline so your timing is good."

He left the program manager's office and stood there in the hot Texas sun. Even though it was May, summer was already on its way in Houston. He put on his sunglasses and acknowledged to himself that his health was the only reason why he'd ever thought of doing this.

He was going to find a way to stay involved in the Cronus program on his own terms. Dennis had offered to find a place for him on his management team, but Ace wasn't ready to accept that he'd be grounded. He had been training to meet the physical challenges of extended spaceflight since he first heard about the mission parameters. And Dennis had done his best to help Ace out, giving him every opportunity to log as much space-time as he could.

Hemi pulled up in his '69 Mustang. The man was a motorhead and spent a lot of his time between missions restoring the car.

"Hop in, Ace. I told the guys you were in town

and we're all meeting over at Rocket Fuel for wings and suds."

Ace was glad Hemi had the top down because it didn't encourage conversation. But they got caught in the lunchtime traffic of workers leaving the base and silence built around them.

"What did you talk to Dennis about?"

Ace filled him in about his plans for the ranch. He wasn't ready to tell the whole base, but he trusted Hemi with his secrets and his life.

"Good. You'd be a great director for the new facility. But I still want you with me on our next mission. I've been thinking about your bone-density issue since you left. I mentioned it to my mom and she sent me—" he broke off to rummage around behind Ace's seat "—this. It's a diet that works to correct osteopenia. I know Doctor Tomlin's on it already, but a little more help can't hurt, right? I even ran it by the doc earlier."

Ace took the email from Hemi and saw that Mona, Hemi's mom, had addressed the body of the email to him.

He smiled as he read over all her notes. She was a holistic healer in California, where she lived with Hemi's dad. And her advice was different from what the program's medical personnel had given him.

"Thanks, man."

"No problem. Mom's afraid if I go up there without you, I'll get into trouble," he said.

Ace had saved Hemi one time during some equipment failure and the other man had never forgotten it. Hemi was the youngest in his family and they were all very protective of their "big warrior."

"I guess everyone's waiting to see if the doctor's

theories about how to fix this pan out," Ace said while they were driving.

Hemi made a grunting noise under his breath. "You bet we are. You're just one of the first who's been out of Earth's gravity that long, but we all need to know that the astronauts will be able to walk and function when they get to the way station and, later, to Mars."

"Exactly. Even though NASA has green-lit the long-term space facility, and has the first long-term mission on the books, if Tomlin's theories aren't proven effective, it could mean…" He trailed off. He didn't want to say it out loud. *The end of the Cronus missions until some sort of solution was found.* Everything was riding on Ace and the three other astronauts who had experienced the effects of prolonged exposure in space and were being monitored by the medical team.

"What about Candice? She's been up there for nine months," Hemi said.

"Tomlin and Dennis didn't say. But I think she's doing well. She's due back on base next week," Ace said. Candice O'Malley was one of the longest-serving female astronauts. The new astronaut classes were more gender-balanced than they had been even ten years earlier when he'd first gone to astronaut training school.

"I'll talk to her when she's back and text you," Hemi said.

"Better to email. The ranch has a really spotty cell phone signal," Ace said.

"That sucks."

"Yes and no. It will be kind of nice to be on the back of a horse working with cattle or on the fence line and have nothing but that chore to focus on. Sort of like being in space. There is no pinging of my phone, no texts coming in fast and furious. Just me and the land."

Hemi turned to look at him, leveling his steady dark gaze at Ace. "Dude, you are starting to sound like…a cowboy."

"I guess I was always one. Just forgot. Dennis thought going back would be the best therapy for me. Give me a chance to do some different work that would build my strength."

"I hope it works," Hemi said. "Not just for you, Ace. I really want this long-term mission to be a go and I know that you and Candice are the ones they are looking at. Dev and Maury are already back in the training schedule, but they weren't up there any longer than I've been."

"I know," Ace said. "Don't talk about this too much."

"I won't," Hemi said. "But most of our training group already has some idea of what is going on. Seeing you today will help them. I think they're afraid you're going to hobble in using a cane. Everyone is excited for the new missions and understands the associated risks, but you know it's different to actually see them. And how you recover is going to affect everyone."

"Well, there's nothing to see here," Ace said. He was the leader of this group of astronauts. Had been since Dennis had started pulling all of them together. Ace knew that today it was important to make each of them believe he was still going to lead them on the first Cronus mission.

Traffic started moving again and Ace realized that as much as the Bar T Ranch felt like home and Mick and Rina had been family, this was where his true family was. And as attracted as he was to Molly, as much as he wanted her, she didn't know him the way Hemi and his fellow astronauts did. But as he ate lunch with the guys and listened to them talking, he also became very aware that his life had been one-dimensional for a long time. Just NASA. Just focused on training. He was surrounded by his astronaut family, but something was calling him back to the Bar T. It wasn't the horses or the other hands… He missed Molly.

JEB DIDN'T SAY anything as she saddled her horse and they rode out to do the afternoon chores. When she'd been a teenager and she'd felt like she was going to scream from frustration at having to rush home from school to help with chores instead of hanging out in town with her friends, her dad had always assigned her to ride with Jeb. There was something calming about Jeb, steady and quiet. He was sure of himself and he rode with an easy grace that came from spending a lifetime in the saddle.

The ranch and ranching business had changed, but Jeb never would.

They fed the cattle and worked quietly alongside each other. And the tightness that had taken up residence in the pit of her stomach loosened. She let the peace of the day and the land wash over her. The sounds of the cattle and the horses.

The rhythm of life on the ranch worked magic on her troubled soul. That was why she never left for long. The land was part of her. She wondered if it was the same for Jason. If being up in his capsule in space soothed something deep inside of him.

Probably.

That was why he'd backed away in the kitchen last night. The sex had been amazing, better than even her steamiest dreams. But they were just having fun. She needed to remember that.

"I needed this," she said to Jeb. There was something reassuring about doing the same chores she'd done for most of her life with Jeb by her side.

"I know."

She shook her head. "Jason made a suggestion that I wasn't expecting when we were at the lawyer's yesterday…using the land for a NASA training facility."

Jeb pushed his straw cowboy hat back on his head. "Say what?"

"I was surprised, too, but I think it could work. NASA would build the facility and we'd still run the ranch on this part of the land. The old bunkhouses would need to be updated—again on NASA's dime— to house the trainees. What do you think?" she asked, realizing maybe she should have talked to Jeb before she'd signed off on the plan.

"Sounds… I'm not sure. I like the idea that we don't have to play cowboys to a bunch of tourists, but a NASA training facility? What do we know about that?"

"Jason is the expert. He said NASA would hire the right people for the roles. Mostly we'd just liaise between the ranch and the facility. He's going to manage most of the details."

"I thought he was going back to space," Jeb said.

"The work we do at the facility will help NASA to determine who goes and who doesn't. It will provide the specialized training astronauts need for long-term missions. Something called Cronus. Jason would have to be evaluated and trained along with the other astronauts."

She didn't want to mention his health issue. It was his story to share if he wanted to.

"So, when will we know about this?"

"Soon, I think. In the meantime we should act as if we're going to win the bid. You've already started clearing the land, which needs to happen regardless, but there's more work that we'll have to do."

"I think the bunkhouses are going to take a while. There is a leak in the southern house. The one where some of the boys used to stay."

"Rina's brother is in construction. I'll ask her to make a call. Maybe they can put their company's name forward when NASA is ready to choose builders."

"Sounds good to me."

"I need you to assign someone to show Jason the acreage that will be used for the facility. He didn't spend much time in that part of the ranch when he lived here before."

"Why don't you show him?" Jeb asked, turning to gaze at the horizon.

"Because I'm busy," she said.

"All right, missy, no need to bite my head off," Jeb said.

"Sorry. I'm just…"

"It's fine. He always did rattle you."

Jeb rode off before she could say anything else. But what would she have said? *No, he doesn't…* Jason made her crazy. Not the good kind, either. Except for last night.

She wished… Why had she been so curt with him when they got back?

Because she'd felt him slipping away.

And it was easier to back away herself than to be the one who was holding on. The one who wanted more than the other was willing to give. She'd done love once. Been burned so badly that she'd retreated here and kept her distance from men ever since.

She needed to remember that. She didn't want to be back at heartbreak hotel again. Rina had patched her up the last time and Molly had vowed she'd be smarter and stronger if she ever met a man she liked again. But it seemed that her heart didn't care about common sense.

She hadn't counted on Jason McCoy. Hadn't figured he'd ever walk through her door again, but here he was. Making plans and promises, and she was just following along. Letting her battered heart hope she could handle whatever the future held.

10

MOLLY WASN'T HAVING the best day. She had thought she'd do anything to save the ranch, but not knowing what was going to happen was making her edgy. She loved the land and had never realized how much she needed it to stay the way it always had been.

Jason wasn't really helping. He had called once in the three days since he'd left to tell her he had gone to Houston and was on his way to San Diego to meet with a defense subcontractor. He made a few bid-related requests. He was all business. How much plainer did things need to be before she got the message? Even though he was trying to move their plan forward, the short call had left her feeling confused and angry. Not at all what she'd expected after their night together.

She wondered if she'd made a huge mistake by partnering with him and starting down this crazy path that would—if he had his way—lead him away from her.

Now, in the middle of her daily tour of the ranch property, she heard odd sounds and she brought Thunder to a stop. Not construction sounds, but something repetitive. *Strange.* As far as she knew, the hands were working elsewhere. The zoning commissioner had stopped by earlier to make sure they could use their land for the NASA facility if the bid was successful, but she was gone now.

Molly dismounted her horse and dropped the reins. knowing Thunder would stay, and then walked closer to the old homestead. It was a ramshackle house that the first Tanner to live on the Bar T had built. He'd brought his mail-order bride to the house. Even though it was in a sad state of disrepair, the beams were still solid and one day Molly hoped to renovate it.

Maybe with the profits from the NASA project, she would.

She wanted to be optimistic about the training facility, but she felt torn. She knew at the heart of her mixed feelings was the knowledge that whatever came of the project, Jason would do everything in his power to get back to active duty. To leave her behind, maybe for good.

She rounded the trail and stopped in her tracks.

The source of the sounds was *Jason*.

Shirtless, with sweat on his torso, he hefted one of the heavy railroad ties that had originally been part of the front porch over his head. He held it there for a count of twelve, his muscles bulging, and she heard him cursing as he counted. Not using the old one-Mississippi but instead one-fucking-damn.

She bit her lower lip to keep from smiling, and as he squatted to lower the beam she stayed where she was. His faded blue jeans rode low on his hips. When he stooped to pick up the beam again the fabric pulled tight against his backside.

Lord, he had a great ass.

He lifted, counting again, muscles straining. She realized that she was watching Ace, not Jason. This man was going on the Cronus missions. He was clearly determined to increase his bone density, whatever it took. She couldn't believe the strength he already possessed.

He had just returned, but he was going to leave her.

She tried to turn to walk away, but her boot heel caught on some trail debris and she let out a shriek as she lost her balance and fell on her backside. Legs and arms akimbo, she wished just once she could have a little bit of grace.

Jason turned, slowly lowering the railroad tie to the ground. He wiped his face where beads of sweat had formed and then sauntered over to her like a man who knew he owned her, body and soul.

She wanted to deny it, even if just to herself, but she knew she couldn't. She pushed herself to her feet and waited for him to get closer. The scent of his earthy musk mingled with his spicy aftershave. She put her hand up, not even pretending she was doing anything other than touching his bulging pecs. He flexed the padded muscles of his chest under her hand.

"Spying on me?"

"Actually, I didn't realize you'd come back."

"But you found me anyway," he said.

"I did," she admitted. "God, you are hot."

"I am sweaty. Is that gross?" he asked.

On any other guy, probably, but on him…no. Not even close.

Molly couldn't resist rubbing her thumb over his flat brown nipple. His eyes widened and his lips parted.

"I'm guessing you don't mind."

Molly didn't want to talk. She was mad at him.

Still. Even more upset with herself for letting him get to her. She'd missed him. She wanted them to have sex again. She'd even gone to see her doctor after that night in her truck and got a prescription for the pill so she wouldn't have to worry about a condom. She figured all the medical tests Jason had been through recently would have turned up any sexually transmitted diseases. And he was the first man she'd been with in a long time.

She stood on her tiptoes, wrapping her arms around his neck and pulling his mouth down to hers. Her tongue brushed his and she closed her eyes without meaning to. She felt him shaking slightly, his control slipping.

She wanted more and refused to deny herself. She took her hand in his, linking their fingers together. His hand in hers was solid and strong.

The sun shone brightly down on them, warming them as he led her toward the shade provided by a large oak tree. Underneath she noticed his sleeping bag.

"So you haven't just returned from San Diego. You've been hiding out," she said.

"Not hiding…just giving you some space," he said.

"I don't need space, Jason," she admitted.

"What do you need?" he asked.

"You."

He drew her into his arms from behind. His head rested on her shoulder and his big hands spanned her waist. She stood completely still, feeling the heat of his body against hers. They fit perfectly together.

He turned her in his arms, keeping his hands at her waist. He gave her a half smile before he leaned in closer.

"You have a very tempting mouth," he said softly, his breath brushing her lips. "It's all can think about."

"Really?"

"Yes. No matter how many weights I lift or how hard I drive my body, exhaustion doesn't seem to quell my need for you."

Then, his mouth was on hers. He took his time kissing her, rubbing his lips lightly over hers. She wanted more and opened her mouth to invite him closer. He tasted so…delicious.

She swept her tongue into his mouth and he met her thrusts with his own. Then he closed his teeth carefully over her tongue and sucked. She shivered and went up on her tiptoes to get closer to him.

His taste was addicting and she wanted more. *Yes*, she thought, she wanted much more of him, not just his kisses.

She put her hands on his shoulders and then moved them higher to rub his scalp. His short hair was soft and smooth under her palms.

His hands drifted to her shoulders, and then past them, his fingers tracing a delicate pattern over her breasts. One brushed the edge of her nipple.

Exquisite shivers racked her body as his finger continued to move slowly over her. He found the buttons and undid them slowly. Once her top was fully unfastened and the material fell away from her, he pushed it down her arms to the ground, taking her wrists in his hands and stepping back.

She was proud of her body and worked hard to stay in shape, and she was very glad of that as he looked at her. His gaze started at the top of her head and moved down her neck and chest to her waist.

His hands followed his gaze, unfastening her bra and drawing it away from her chest. He dropped it to the ground before he wrapped his hands around her waist, lifting her. "Wrap your legs around me."

She did and immediately she was surrounded by him. His hands were on her butt, his mouth was on her breasts and he suckled her gently. Nibbling at her nipples as he massaged her backside. When he took one nipple into his mouth, she felt everything inside of her tighten and her center grow moist.

Then he laid her down on the soft sleeping bag and knelt over her. His mouth… She couldn't even think. She could only feel the sensations that were washing over her as he continued to focus on her breasts.

One of his heavy thighs parted her legs and then he was between them. She felt the ridge of his cock rubbing against her core and she shifted to increase the sensation.

She wanted to touch him, had to hold him to her as he kissed his way from her breasts down to her belly button. He looked up at her and for a moment when their eyes met there was something in his that alarmed her. He wanted her, but he didn't want to want her, she thought.

She only let it disturb her for a second before he lowered his head again and nibbled at the skin of her belly, his tongue moving around the indentation of her belly button. Each time he dipped his tongue in, her clit tingled.

His mouth moved lower on her, his hands going to the waistband of her jeans, undoing the button and then slowly lowering the zipper. She felt the warmth of his breath on her lower belly and then the edge of his tongue as he traced the skin revealed by the opening.

His lips felt soft and smooth against her. She moaned a little, afraid to say his name out loud. Afraid he'd hear how much she needed him, wanted him... cared for him.

"Lift your hips," he said.

She planted her feet on the sleeping bag, doing as he'd asked, and felt him draw her jeans over her hips and down her thighs. She was left wearing the tiny black thong she'd put on that morning.

He palmed her through the fabric and she squirmed.

He gave it to her. Running his fingers under her panties to skim her damp flesh. Then he pulled her underwear down with his teeth. He leaned back on his knees and just stared down at her.

"You are exquisite," he said.

His voice was low and husky and made her blood flow heavier in her veins. Everything about this man seemed to make her hotter and hornier than she'd ever been before.

"It's you," she said in a raspy voice. "You are the one who is making me..."

"I *am* making you," he said. "And I'm not going to be happy until you come harder than you ever have before."

She shuddered at the impact of his words. She felt them all the way through her body. He lowered his head again and rubbed his chin over her. The stubble brushing against her sensitive clit was sweet torment.

He parted her with the thumb and forefinger of his left hand and she felt the air against her flesh and then the pressure of his tongue. It was so firm and wet and she squirmed again, wanting—no, needing—more from him.

He scraped his teeth over her and she almost came right then, but he lifted his head and smiled up her body at her. It was becoming clear that Jason was the kind of lover who wanted to draw out the experience.

She gripped his shoulders as he teased her with his mouth and then she tunneled her fingers through his hair, holding him closer as she lifted her hips. He moaned against her and the sound tickled her clit and sent chills racing through her body.

One hand traced the opening of her body. Those large deft fingers made it impossible to stay still. Her breasts felt full and her nipples were tight as he pushed just the tip of his finger inside of her.

The first ripples of her orgasm started to pulse through her, but he pulled back again, lifting his head and moving down her body, nibbling at the flesh of her legs. She was aching for him.

"Jason…"

"Yes?" he asked, lightly stroking her lower belly and then moving both hands to cup her breasts.

"I need more."

"You will get it," he said.

"Now."

He shook his head. "That's not the way to get what you want. I'm in charge this afternoon, Molly."

She was shivering with the need to come and wanted his big body moving over hers. Wanted his cock inside of her. She reached between them and stroked him through his pants, then slowly lowered the tab of the zipper. He caught her wrist and raised her hand above her head.

"That's not what I had in mind," she said.

He lowered his body over hers so the muscled hardness of his chest brushed her breasts. Then, his thigh was between her legs, moving slowly against her engorged flesh, and she wanted to cry out as everything in her tightened just a little bit more.

She writhed against him, but he just slowed his touch so that the sensations were even more intense than before. He shifted again and she felt the warmth of his breath against her clit. She opened her eyes to look down at him and this time she knew she saw something different. But she couldn't process it because his mouth was on her.

He plunged a finger deep inside her at the same time and she moaned his name. The first wave of orgasm rolled through her body.

Her hips jerked forward. She felt the moisture between her legs and his finger pushing hard against her G-spot. She was shivering and her entire body was convulsing, but he didn't lift his head. He kept sucking and driving her harder and harder until she came again, screaming with her orgasm as stars danced behind her eyelids.

Pleasure overcame her. It was more than she could process and she had to close her eyes. She reached for Jason, needing some sort of comfort after that storm of pleasure, but he was gone.

She was still shivering and her pulse was racing as she opened her eyes and found him staring right into them and leaning back. She reached for his zipper and freed him. Took him into her hands and then drew him forward as she parted her legs.

"Damn. I don't have a condom."

"I'm on the pill," she said. The words were raw, needy and husky.

He shifted his hips and plunged deep into the heart of her. She wrapped her legs and arms around him. Held on as tightly as she could. Hoped he'd never realize just how much she wanted him. And not just for the afternoon...

11

FIVE WEEKS PASSED quickly on the ranch after their afternoon of hot sex. Keeping busy, Jason and Molly hadn't seen much of each other, except when they needed to discuss business. Jason was working with Jeb and Andy, the ranch hand that Jeb had assigned to him. The land had been cleared and next week they'd hear about their bid. Dennis had been tight-lipped about it. But Lynn, who was the director of Axiom Space Systems—the defense subcontractor Ace had met in San Diego whom they'd decided to partner with—said that was normal. Her people thought their bid was strong and that they would be awarded the contract. But there was no way to know until next week.

Jason had been working out and eating more healthy than he normally did, but his body had to be in the best shape possible for the medical evaluation that was scheduled in another six weeks. Three months had seemed like an eternity originally, but it was flying by. Well, the days were. The nights were long. Plagued with dreams of Molly and those damned long legs of hers. He woke up hard and sweating every night. He knew all he had to do was walk down the hall and knock on her door…but he was afraid of what her reaction to be.

And he wasn't sure what scared him more, the possibility of her turning him away or inviting him in.

She'd changed him. Woken something that he'd never realized was inside of him. And for the first time in his life he was conflicted about NASA. He'd never been afraid of anything before, but now he wasn't sure. He didn't know if he wanted to go back to space, to leave her for eighteen months. He was starting to think of himself as Jason again, not Ace. So he'd stayed in his own bed, fire burning inside of him each night, making him hungrier for her each day.

"There's a call for you on the ranch phone," Andy said as he bounced to a stop next to him on the Mule. The Mule was an all-terrain vehicle similar to the one Mick had been driving when he'd had his accident.

"Can I call them back?" Jason asked. "It's going to take a while for me to return to the house."

"No. It's urgent. That's why I'm here. I'll take care of your horse. You take the Mule."

Andy got out of the ATV and Jason got in. He drove it expertly across the bumpy ground. It wasn't that different from some of the training he'd done at NASA for maneuvering vehicles on foreign surfaces. This was one of part of the program that the ranch was going to develop to get astronauts ready for Mars.

If the call was urgent…well, he'd better get there as quickly as he could. He drove past the barn where he normally would have parked the Mule and pulled up to the house.

He hopped out of the vehicle and bounded up the steps.

Molly and Rina stopped talking as he entered the kitchen. Molly had her hair up and he flashed back to when he'd kissed her neck. That sweet spot where her pulse had been beating so strongly. She wasn't wearing any makeup, but her lips looked full and her mouth so…addicting. He was going to crack, unable to resist the lure of Molly much longer.

The worst part was that she wasn't doing anything. She was just being friendly…

"I have a call?"

"Yes. It's Dennis Lock. He said it was urgent," she said. "You can take it on the extension in the den."

"Thanks," he said, walking past both women down the hall to Mick's den. As he entered he realized the room was slowly becoming Molly's. There were little touches that hadn't been there when it had been Mick's domain.

Things like a scented candle on the credenza. And the pile of papers that had always been stacked precariously on the edge of the desk had been cleared off. A framed picture of Molly and Mick had taken its place.

Jason wiped his hands on his jeans before leaning on the desk and lifting the handset.

"McCoy here."

"Ace. Took long enough. One thing we have to do once you win the bid is get a cell tower put in. It feels like the dark ages when I have to call a landline."

Jason smiled to himself, suppressing a chuckle. "It is a different world out here."

"I bet. I have two pieces of news. The decision has been made for the facility and my sources said I'll be happy. You should hear something informal today. I'd call Lynn."

"Will do, sir. What's the other news?" he asked.

"I need you back here for an interim medical evaluation. They are pressuring us to name a commander for the first mission and I want it to be you. Doctor Tomlin needs to see if you are making enough progress."

Jason rubbed his chest as, for the first time, he worried he might not be physically able. His body was the one thing he'd always taken for granted. Even when his mom had died and he'd been left on his own, he'd been healthy.

"Okay. What if I'm not?"

"Don't even think it," Dennis said.

"You'll have to name someone else, won't you?"

There was silence on the line for a long minute and Jason felt a burst of anger. *Dammit.*

"Hemi's good," Jason said finally.

"He is, but he's not ready. Not yet. I want you, Ace. But we won't send you to space if we can't bring you back whole."

"Fair enough. I can't get down to Houston today. Can I come tomorrow?"

"Yes. Call Lynn first and then Tomlin. She's going to want to set up a series of exercises and tests."

Dennis finished the call and Ace hung up the phone but didn't leave the room. He didn't make the other calls he needed to make. He glanced down at his body. He'd been working out every day and he felt like he was in the best shape of his life. But he had no idea if his bone density had improved. *Hell.* He wanted to punch something. He wanted…

There was a knock on the door.

"Who is it?"

"Molly."

Yeah, that was what he wanted.

MOLLY HAD KEPT Jason at arm's length as much as pos-sible during the last five weeks, burying herself in work. Done the smart thing. But she wasn't too sure how much longer she could do it. Hence, standing out-side her own den door, knocking.

She'd seen the look on Jason's face when Dennis's name had been mentioned. She thought they'd have a little more time before NASA made a decision about the facility, so maybe instead this was…news about Jason and the space program.

She'd stood outside this door more than once. When she'd set herself on fire in the barn, Dad had taken her to town for emergency treatment and then when she'd come home and was healthy again, he'd told her to meet him here. She'd known she was in trouble…

This time it was Jason in trouble. Not her. She felt it. She had no idea what kind of news he'd gotten, but she heard banked anger in his voice on the phone and she told herself it wasn't her problem.

She could just walk away and no one would blame her. Jason wouldn't blame her or expect anything else from her, but she couldn't do that. No matter how much she'd been trying to think of their lovemaking as sexy fun, she cared about him. Always had.

She'd spent most of her teenaged years pretending that he was just another one of her dad's boys. But he never had been. She couldn't lie about that. Her heart wasn't fickle.

She opened the door. He sat there on the edge of her desk. The look he gave her was desperate and dark.

It hadn't been good news.

Of course, it hadn't. Good news wasn't usually urgent.

"Want to talk?"

He shook his head.

"Want to be alone?" she asked.

"No. Molly, I don't want to be alone," he said slowly, emphasizing each word.

"What do you want?" she asked.

"You. No more pretending. Can you do that? If not, turn around and leave. Give me some time to get my head back to the polite place I've been in for the last few weeks," he said.

She stood there. She should walk away. That would be the smart thing to do. This wasn't the sweet Jason who seduced her with barbecue sandwiches and stories. This was a man who was broken and he needed something raw from her.

God, she wanted to give it to him. She wasn't going to leave him alone. She closed the door behind her and then leaned against it, her hands behind her back.

He looked down at the floor.

"Leave, Molly. I'm not the nicest guy right now."

"I can't," she admitted. "I've been trying to pretend that all the little things that make you the man you are haven't affected me, but they have. I can't keep ignoring it."

He lifted his head and in those light blue eyes of his she saw so much emotion. Anger, agony, fear and need.

Focus on the need, she told herself and subtly locked the door behind her as she took a step forward. Rina sometimes just let herself in and Molly didn't want to be interrupted. Not now.

She toed off her boots, noticed that Jason shifted on the desk to face her. "What are you doing?"

"Not leaving."

"I can see that."

"Well, I think you're smart enough to figure out what I'm doing…"

She tugged off her socks, too, and stopped where she was. "Unless you really do want me to leave."

"No. Don't go."

He opened his arms and she smiled at him.

She pulled her T-shirt up over her head and tossed it aside, hearing his breath catch.

She stopped to look at him. He'd said he liked her appearance and in his eyes she read the truth of those words. The way he watched her was the way…well, the way she'd seen men look at underwear models.

She felt the power of being a woman. At this moment she held Jason captive and she wanted to make the moment last. She wanted to make him forget whatever was troubling him.

"Like this?"

"I do. I'd like it better if you took off your bra," he said.

"I might. But first you are going to have to show me something. Maybe that strong chest of yours."

"You like my muscles?"

"I do. They turn me on. And when I see you flex your biceps…it takes my breath away."

"It does?" he asked, slowly undoing the buttons of his work shirt and letting the sides fall open.

He left the shirt on with just about two inches of

lean masculine chest visible. Her fingers tingled with the need to touch him and she took a step closer. She was trying to be seductive, but she didn't want to wait any longer. The truth was, she knew what she wanted. And it wasn't all this distance between them.

He held his hand up. "Wait. Take your hair down."

She reached up, pulled the hair tie free and shook her head as her hair fell around her shoulders. She took another step forward.

He just watched her. His eyes were half closed, but she knew she held all of his attention. She put her hand in the center of his chest. He had a light dusting of hair there and she ran her fingers through it. She pushed on his chest and he leaned back on his elbows, causing his shirt to fall away from his body. She reached underneath it, wrapping her arms around him and resting her head over his heart. Just for a minute she wanted the comfort of his body. Then the heat that flowed between them demanded her attention. This wasn't about comfort. This was about raw need. Just Molly and Jason and nothing else.

She pushed his shirt down his arms and he sat up to shrug out of it, then tossed it aside. Pressing him back until he was sitting on the desk, she climbed onto his lap. She tunneled her fingers through his close-cropped hair, drawing his mouth toward hers. Then she sucked his bottom lip between her teeth and kissed him slowly. Taking her time to explore him.

She shifted back, resting her butt on his thighs as she nibbled her way down his neck and chest. His nipples were flat and hard. He caught her hand, lifted it to his mouth and kissed the center of it. Shivers spread up her arm causing her own nipples to harden.

He reached behind her with his other hand and unfastened her bra. He took her hand, the one he'd just kissed, and placed it over her own breast. It felt exotic and turned her on to feel her own nipple hardening under her palm as he guided her hand.

She shifted on his lap and, reaching around his back with her other hand, feathered her fingers up and down his spine, dipping them beneath the waistband of his jeans to touch the slight indents at the top of his firm ass.

He arched his back and she felt his erection growing between them. She repositioned again so she could rub her center over the ridge of his cock as she kissed him. He kept moving their hands over her breast and she responded to that touch, rubbing herself more fully against him.

He moaned and she smiled to herself as his hips jerked forward slightly. She used her free hand to reach between them and unfasten his jeans, drawing the zipper carefully down over his erection.

He put his hands on her waist and lifted her off him, setting her on her feet next to the desk. He stood up next to her and undid her jeans, pushing them and her panties slowly down her legs. Then he moved behind her and slipped her bra straps over her shoulders, letting it fall to the ground.

She glanced back at him. Let her eyes move slowly down his body. He was so strong and muscled everywhere. He was thick and proud. She tried to turn, to reach for him, but he stopped her. He tangled one of his hands in her hair and nudged her forward. She leaned on the desk, arching her back as he hovered over her. She felt his lips on the back of her neck and then he nibbled his way down her back, still holding her hair in one of his hands.

She shifted, pressing back toward him, hoping to feel his cock against her, but he kept his hips back. His free hand traveled down the side of her breast, making her nipple bead. She squirmed, desperate for more contact, but he just moved his hand farther down the side of her body.

She felt his fingers on her butt cheek, grabbing and squeezing. She was wet and needy. More ready for him than she'd ever been for any man.

She tried to turn her head, but he held her where she was. She felt him against her back as he leaned over her. He whispered dark, sexy words into her ear, telling her in detail everything he wanted to do to her. And then she felt him poised at the entrance of her body.

He grunted and she gasped in pleasure as he penetrated her in one swift move, pushing forward until he was fully seated. He was so deep. She moaned and tightened around him.

He drew his hips back and entered her again, harder this time. She met his thrust, pressing back from the desk so that their hips slammed together, bringing him even deeper.

He braced one hand next to her head on the desk and she bit his wrist as he pulled back and then starting thrusting, his powerful legs and hips and his long, hard cock driving her higher and higher, closer to her climax. His hand twisted in her hair and she cried out his name as her orgasm took her by surprise.

He picked up speed, losing control as he continued thrusting, the friction exciting her all over again. She heard her name on his lips and felt him empty himself inside her as a second orgasm washed over her. He collapsed on her back. Keeping his weight off her, he dropped soft kisses between her shoulder blades and she lay there, let her eyes close.

He didn't say anything, just held her in his arms and that was all she needed. Or at least she was going to pretend that was enough. But she knew she wasn't going to want to sleep alone now. Whatever happened with Jason and his future, she needed more of this... more of him.

12

"WANT TO TALK?" Molly asked as they were sitting in the large tub in her bathroom en suite.

"No," he said. "But we probably should."

"That isn't very reassuring," she said.

He rubbed her arm, unable to stop himself from touching her. They'd gathered their clothes from the den and had run up the stairs and into her room like naughty kids. The bathtub had seemed a logical place to end up together. She was leaning on his chest, their feet propped up on the other end of the tub. Her feet with their purple toenails looked especially tiny between his larger ones.

Reassuring… He wasn't sure he had ever known how to be that man, but right now he wasn't feeling it. He was more lost than he'd been after the first evaluation.

"Good news first."

"Okay," she said.

"We might have won the bid for the facility," he said. "I'm supposed to call Lynn. Dennis got some insider news that he'd be happy with the winner of the bid. He thinks that means us."

"Good," she said. "Jeb is getting pretty excited about the facility and the land's ready for construction now."

"Yeah. He told me that if he'd been better at science, he would have tried to become an astronaut. Flying's in his blood. His old man was a fighter pilot in Vietnam."

"Really?" Molly asked. "I never knew that."

Jason knew he was stalling, but he didn't want to say out loud that he might not make the cut for the program. That his space dreams might be over when they'd barely started. And he knew that wasn't fair. He'd spent way more time among the stars than most other astronauts had, but he wanted more. He needed more.

Molly put her hand on his wrist, drew it up her body and kissed his knuckles. "Just say it. Whatever your bad news is. It's not going to get better keeping it to yourself."

She was right. He knew that, but once he said it… "Dennis is being pressured to name the commander for the first mission. He wants me, but I'm still grounded. He asked me to come to Houston and take a slew of tests to see if I've made improvements. If I have, he will push back, say he wants me and that I'm recovering."

"If not, he'll name someone else," she said, filling in the rest. "That sucks. So when do you have to go?"

"Tomorrow. I've done everything I can."

"I know. What's the process?" she asked.

"Usually, they have us do a series of blood tests and then spend many hours in a specialized room where they can see how being in a zero gravity simulation affects the body."

Molly turned in the tub so she could face him. She put her hands on his shoulders and looked into his eyes.

"At least you'll know," she said.

"I don't want to," he said at last. "I wanted the full three months so that I could be further along in my recovery from the yearlong mission."

"What can you do?" she asked.

"Nothing. Dennis said it best—they don't want to bring me back in pieces." Jason was trying to make it sound like a joke, but he couldn't. He didn't want to give up on being a part of the Cronus missions.

She shook her head. "It's not funny."

"I know. If I don't laugh, I think I'm going to cry."

"Do you want me to go to Houston with you?" she asked.

He hadn't thought of bringing anyone along. All of his adult life he'd been on his own. By choice, he realized, because Mick might have been more involved in his life if he'd asked him. "I would like that. Can you be away from the ranch?"

"I don't see why not. Jeb says I get in his way."

Jason could imagine Jeb saying that, but they both knew how important her work on the ranch was. "I won't be able to spend much time with you. I mean, I'll be in the testing facility for the most part."

"It's okay. I want to see the space center and do some more research on the kind of training we'll be providing if our bid goes through. When are we going to call Lynn?"

"Not until we get out of this tub. Are you excited about the facility?"

She turned back around, settling against his chest once again. "I am. It's different and we haven't done anything new here in forever."

"Nervous at all?"

"I'm more nervous about going to Houston with you."

He squeezed her close. "Why?"

"Everyone will know we're together," she said. "Or assume it. And you know how the ranch is…so gossipy. Once you leave—"

"If I leave. This is going to be the trip that makes the difference, Molly. This test will decide my future."

She tipped her head back to look up at him. "You will decide your future. The test is going to just point out the possibilities."

"That's very wise," he said.

"Dad said the same thing to me. When I dropped out of college, I said, 'I guess I have no choice except ranching.' He told me I had the same choices I'd always had. I'd simply eliminated one possibility."

Mick had been such a good dad, Jason thought. As long as he'd known him, the older man had always had a long vision of the future. It was hard to imagine the world without him in it, but Mick lived on in Molly and in everyone whose life he'd touched.

"I miss him. I could use his advice right now," Jason said.

"He'd say something ambiguous and make you think he'd told you something wise," she said. "Then you'd make your decision and he'd nod like you were the smartest person in the world. God, I miss that. He could make me feel like I'd chosen correctly with one nod."

"Because you knew he had your back," Jason said.

"Exactly. Well, whatever happens, I have your back, Ace."

"THAT MEANS MORE than you can know," he said.

She didn't elaborate. Didn't tell him she wanted him to stay. Even when she'd been keeping her distance, every moment he'd been back on the Bar T had just made her fall a little more for him. There was something about Jason. It wasn't good looks—though he was very handsome in a rugged, sexy sort of way. It was something deeper.

The way he'd jumped right in and taken on all the ranch's problems and helped her come up with a plan. Granted, it was a plan she couldn't have executed without him, but he'd done something. He hadn't just stood by and waited to see what she could do.

She hadn't needed him to save her, but it was nice to have him by her side. She guessed some might say she was projecting the feelings she'd had for her dad onto Jason. Though she didn't really know him any better than she had when he'd left the ranch as a teenager, she knew that there was more between them.

A lot more. And it wasn't just the sex, even if that was amazing.

"What will you do if you can't go back into space?" she asked. His hands were moving restlessly on her body, almost as if he was absently caressing her.

"I haven't thought much about it. I think Dennis would give me a role in management if I wanted it, or

I could take on more responsibility training the other astronauts at the facility."

"Would you do that?" To her it seemed like the worst kind of torture for him to be close to something he wanted but would never be able to have.

"I guess. I can't imagine being grounded permanently."

"I'm sorry," she said.

"Don't be. I haven't taken the medical yet."

THE WATER HAD started to cool, but Ace didn't want to let Molly go. Not yet. He stood up, lifting her with him and put her on her feet next to the tub.

"What are you doing?"

"I'm not ready to get out yet, but it's getting cold," he said.

He bent over to drain and then refill the tub. He felt her fingers tracing the last part of his tattoo, the word *go*. "You are very bold," she said.

"Why?"

"Because you test your limits in space, for everyone's benefit. You don't let anything stand in your way, do you?"

"Not for the things I love," he said, glancing over his shoulder at her.

She was gazing at his side, biting her lower lip, and her fingers were lightly moving over him. She looked...sad again. He had made it clear from the beginning that he had one foot in this world on the ranch and the other in his gravity boots, ready for the next mission, but that didn't make it any easier for her, he imagined. He knew it wasn't easy for him.

"You don't love very much, do you?" she asked,

glancing up, blushing when she realized he was watching her.

"No. I'm discerning. A bit like you, I'd say."

She nodded, dropping her hand to walk over to the shelf where she kept the scented bath salts. He considered it lucky that he wasn't going to Houston until tomorrow. Her salts and bubble bath were both lavender-scented. And while the smell was soothing, he didn't even want to contemplate the ribbing he'd get from the other guys if he showed up smelling like flowers.

She dumped a small handful of the salts in the bath and then looked over at him.

"What?"

How could he put into words that just watching her move turned him on? The last five weeks had been long. Too long. He had dreamed of her each night and had then been tortured during the day as he'd watched her just going about her routine. There was something inherently sexy about everything she did.

He shrugged.

He didn't want to say anything that would make the situation between them even more impossible than it already was.

He wanted her. He liked her. He wanted to protect her. But he was leaving. No matter what, he was going to find a way to go on the Cronus missions and if he let her get any closer, it would be harder to leave.

He flicked off the faucets as the water reached the correct level and then turned his back on her. Didn't want to look into her eyes with that knowledge in his own.

He held his hand out to her and she took it hesitantly.

"Are you okay?" she asked.

"Yes," he said. If he said it enough, maybe the words would eventually become true. Faking it. He'd been faking it for so long, trying to be like the men who had inspired him. Like Mick, here on the ranch—acting like there wasn't anything he didn't know. Like Dennis at the space center—pretending that nothing about the universe and the unknown scared him. And…well, like every image of the perfect lover, for her. He wanted to give her everything when inside he wasn't sure he had that much to give.

"Kiss me," he said. He needed to be lost in her. Lost in her kiss, which had the power to make him stop thinking and just feel alive and complete. He felt like he was enough when she was in his arms.

She stepped closer, pressing her naked body to his and wrapping her arms around his torso. Leaning back for a moment, she kissed the center of his chest then moved to the left, tracing his tattoo with her tongue. Then she looked up at him. Their eyes met and he realized he wasn't fooling her.

The expression in her eyes seemed as ageless as the land the Bar T sat on and as vast as the universe he wanted to explore. Sometimes he honestly felt like everything he'd ever been searching for was found in her.

"You boldly go," she said. "Don't forget that, Ace. You came from the streets and made it to the stars. Nothing is going to keep you grounded. Not your bone-density problems, not this ranch and, I promise you, not me."

He couldn't speak as emotions grabbed him by the throat. He tangled his hands in her hair and brought his mouth down hard on hers. The kiss was intense and powerful. A punishment, because she saw too much of him. Saw too clearly what he didn't want anyone to see. But there was no hiding from Molly.

Holy hell. When had she slipped past his guard? When had that happened?

Her fingernails dug into his side and she bit his tongue lightly, returning the fervor of the embrace.

He pulled his head back, looked down into her eyes and wished he hadn't. The intensity in her gaze made him realize that she already cared more than was wise.

He wished for a minute that he was a different person. The kind who could see this health thing as a chance to change directions, but he wasn't that man. He'd given his soul to NASA a long time ago and he realized that Molly was okay with that. She knew who he was and she expected him to break her heart.

That should be enough to make him leave the bathroom en suite right now. Get dressed, head to Houston and never come back. That kind of unconditional acceptance would have scared him before—it still sort of did—but what Molly couldn't know was that he felt an equal draw to her. So instead he put his hands on that tiny waist of hers and lifted her off her feet.

He put her down in the deep tub that was filled with bubbles and smelled like summer. Like a summer that wouldn't end but was flying by. It had been just over six weeks since he'd first arrived at the ranch; in six more weeks this would be over. He got in, too, and sat down, the water rising to his chest and sloshing over the sides as he cradled her in his arms. She kissed his arm lightly. He wanted her, wanted the sunshine of Molly and not just the vastness he'd always used to define who he was.

She shifted more, but he held her where she was. He wanted this time with her to last forever. This moment when everything was still possible. She was curled against him and, when she moved her legs, he felt her thigh brush his cock and his blood started to feel as if it were flowing more heavily in his veins.

In response, she turned around to straddle him. She watched him with those serious eyes of hers. And he realized that, though she'd said she was lost six weeks ago, she wasn't anymore.

She had found her peace in the land around them. While he'd been running and planning, she'd found her strength.

She put her hands on his shoulders and twined her legs around his body, locking her ankles behind him.

"This is better. I can see you," she said.

"How is that better?" he asked.

"I want to know what's going on with you. I want to see your face when I move against you. I need to know that I affect you the same way you affect me."

With that, she took the loofah sponge from the pretty porcelain bath tray and submerged it. Bringing it up, she rubbed it over his chest, then from shoulder to shoulder and down his sternum.

She followed the line of hair on his chest until it disappeared under the water. Somehow the loofah got lost. Instead, he felt her fingers on his abdomen and then lower, rubbing his cock until it was hard and he wanted something other than her hands on him.

His hands were restlessly moving up and down her body. Caressing that scar on the inside of her thigh and then moving higher. He loved the way her hips felt as he used both hands to squeeze her and move her on his lap. The tip of his cock brushed against her center, but he took his time, not entering her yet. Finding the loofah floating near him, he picked it up and rubbed it over her shoulders and then down to her nipples, abrading both of them until they were erect. He carefully washed the soapy water off her breasts and then took the tip of one of them between his teeth, lightly biting down on it before sucking it more deeply into his mouth. Her hand on his cock tightened in response.

This was the one place where there was no confusion. When he had her in his arms, nothing seemed complicated. This was all he wanted. She was all he wanted.

He grasped one of her buttocks in his hand as he continued to suck on her nipple, feathering his finger along the crack and feeling her arch against him. Then she put her hands in his hair as she sank lower, rubbing against the shaft of his cock.

She reached between them, adjusting him until he was poised at her entrance. Then she put her hands on his face, forcing his head back, and brought her mouth down hard on his as she shifted and slowly took him into her body. She rocked forward, sinking down until he was deep inside her.

She continued to move her mouth over his and he felt like he did just before the rocket blasted off. Like he was going to explode if she didn't move.

He gripped her butt in both hands as he drew his hips back and then pulled her back down again. They rocked together, both reaching for climax. The water sloshed around them, her wet hair stuck to his neck and their mouths fused together. He drove himself higher and higher inside of her. She rode him harder and faster until he felt her nails dig into his shoulders and she ripped her mouth from his to cry out his name.

Her cries made something tighten inside of him and everything in his body jerked as he started to come. He thrust into her harder and deeper until he emptied himself. As she collapsed against his chest and he held her to him, he knew he could no longer hide the truth from himself. Molly Tanner had changed him.

13

THIS TIME WHEN the water got cold, Molly got out of the tub before Jason. He followed her a moment later, wrapping a towel around his lean hips. He gave her a kiss and left the room, but she stayed in there for a long time getting dressed and thinking about Houston.

Maybe she shouldn't have volunteered to go with him, but she'd heard the loneliness in his voice. He was used to being alone, had told her that he liked it, but this was one instance when she knew he wouldn't want to be.

She took her small Nike duffle bag from the back of her closet and tossed some clothes into it before going downstairs to find Rina.

She was sitting on the back porch drinking a glass of iced tea and talking on the phone. She hung up when she saw Molly.

"What's up, sunshine?"

"I'm going to Houston with Jason," she said. "Just for a few days."

"Well…is there something else you want to tell me?"

She looked over at Rina. She was the closest thing

that Molly had to an aunt and she knew all of Molly's secrets. "We've slept together. I...I care for him."

"Obviously. What's up?"

"I'm not sure what I'm doing. He is going to do everything he can to go back to space. There is no woman alive who can compete with that."

"Don't compete," Rina said. "Why do you have to? You wouldn't leave the ranch to permanently go to Houston, would you?"

"No. I can handle a few days, but my home is here."

Rina sat up, pushing her sunglasses up onto her head. "I imagine it's the same for him."

"I don't know how to do this. In my head...well, I always thought if I fell for a guy, he'd be the type to raise cattle and kids. Not leave the planet for more than a year at a time."

Molly sat down next to Rina on the lounge chair and her friend hugged her. "The heart isn't like that. You might think you want one thing, but you really want something else."

"Why does it have to be that way?"

Rina shrugged. "Girl, you know I'm single and have the worst taste in men. You've seen me crying over a guy or trying to drink his memory away more than once."

"I have," Molly said. "But I always figured I was smarter than you."

Rina lightly punched her arm. "Watch it."

"I just hoped... Should I stay home?"

"Only you can decide. Why did he ask you to go to Houston?" Rina asked.

"Actually, I volunteered. He has to take a test earlier than he anticipated and if he doesn't pass it he may not be chosen to lead the Cronus missions. If he does, I guess he won't be around here too much longer."

"Well, hell. You know how to pick the wrong time to fall for a guy," Rina said.

"Tell me about it. What if I only fall for guys who can't or don't want to be with me? That would suck."

"It would, but Jason does want to be with you."

"You think?" she asked.

"I know. For the last six weeks, every time you entered a room he stopped what he was doing and watched you until you left."

"I think that might have been lust. We were trying to keeping our hands off each other." Pretending that they were fine with the status quo.

Rina slung her arm around Molly's shoulders again. "I've seen attraction and it was more than that. He smiles when you laugh. Listens to your voice even when you aren't speaking to him. He likes you."

But did he like her enough? That was the question that kept spinning around her mind. And would Jason *liking* her even satisfy her? She wasn't going to lie to herself. She was falling for Jason. Falling hard.

She worried that the time they'd spent together didn't seem real to him. The ranch wasn't his life. Being back here must feel like he was pretending. Was she just a diversion to help keep his mind off the outcome of his medical tests and his future?

She wanted him to be part of her future. To build something together that they could share. But she wasn't too sure that was what Jason wanted.

Hell, she was almost positive it wasn't. If he couldn't go on any more missions and decided to stay on the ranch, would she always feel like his consolation prize?

JASON CALLED LYNN to find out if she'd heard anything
from her sources. She had heard the same thing Dennis
had, which she thought meant good news for their bid.
But she said she'd been in the business long enough to
know that anything could happen before the official
announcement. Still, she felt confident enough to book
a trip to Houston and the ranch in four days' time to
assess the property. She liked to meet the people she'd
be working with in person.

Jason hung up and went to look for Molly. He
couldn't find her in the house and Rina was deep in
conversation with Jeb and Andy in the kitchen, so
Jason skipped going in there. He really didn't want to
talk to anyone. Just needed to find Molly.

He didn't like that he felt that way and almost turned
around and went back up to his room. He needed Molly
now. He knew that this afternoon in the office and
the tub had strengthened the tenuous bonds between
them, but it was more than that. He'd needed her for
a while. He depended on being able to talk to her and
get her opinion.

He was using her to help him through this time
when nothing was certain. He knew that wasn't fair,
but that didn't change the truth.

Giving up on his search of the house, he strode outside. The Mule was still parked where he'd left it so he
drove it over to the barn to park it properly and then
sat there listening to the sound of the wind blowing
over the fields. The cattle were all out to pasture, but
the horses in the barn made some soft sounds.

He closed his eyes and stored this moment in his
head. He was determined to go back into space, where
it was cold and he wouldn't hear the wind or smell the

fields. Where he would be isolated again, from everything but his crewmates.

He craved that isolation. As much as he knew he'd miss this, too.

If he passed the medical.

And if he didn't? Would it be enough to stay on the ranch, to run the training facility? Would he still feel whole?

He got off the Mule and walked over to the barn. He glanced inside, but Molly wasn't there. Where had she gone?

He wondered if she'd changed her mind about going with him to Houston.

He'd be disappointed if she had. He shouldn't let this continue, he knew. Shouldn't let himself care for her. He needed to be the Ace he'd always been. And he'd always been on his own. Was he hedging his bets with Molly, keeping her close as a backup plan?

He'd wondered about that before and now it seemed more important that he try to answer the question.

He left the barn and walked back toward the house on the meandering path that took him past the bunkhouses. Only one was being used right now by the hands. They'd set up a basketball hoop to the left of the bunkhouse and three of the guys were playing a game of keep-away.

He remembered growing up here. Remembered playing basketball with the other guys who had found themselves living on the ranch. One of them had called it the ass end of nowhere. It had certainly felt that way to Jason. Mick had been the person who'd made it tolerable for him. Had given him books to read and nur-

tured his love of the cosmos. It was Mick who'd put
the idea of being an astronaut in his head.

That was what he'd thought would happen this
time—returning to the ranch would give him clar-
ity, help him figure out what was next. But it didn't.
He wasn't resetting. He felt too old to start over and
he didn't want to.

He knew what he wanted.

Space.

Exploring the universe, seeing comets, stars, as-
teroids and planets no other human had been close to.

But he also wanted Molly.

This afternoon had made him realize that he wasn't
on a solo mission anymore. Sometime in the last six
weeks that had changed. And it wasn't because of anything she'd been doing. It was because of his own
actions—working on the ranch and making plans for
a life that included NASA but wasn't devoted solely
to it. He'd never had this before and he felt like he had
on his first space walk.

Scared.

Maybe a little bit excited, but unsure, feeling his
way. A part of him was ready to hear that he was permanently grounded.

He was trying to convince himself it would be okay.
Whatever Dr. Tomlin said he'd accept it. He had no
choice.

He neared the house and noticed Molly standing
on the porch, staring down at him. How long had she
been watching him?

What did she see when she looked at him?

A man who was here for the long haul or someone
who was using the Bar T the way he had as a kid? That

would be a fair assessment since he'd been clear that that was what he was doing. But he wanted her to see something better in him.

He wasn't sure what he wanted from her. Hell, he didn't even know what he wanted from himself.

"Whatcha doing?" he called out when he was close enough for her to hear. Trying to be cool and casual. Not like a man who needed her more than he wanted to admit to himself.

"Watching the sky. I think we might get some storms tonight."

He felt like the storm was already here. Raining and thundering through his soul and leaving him huddled and unsure. She watched him and it did nothing to help him. He knew he had to figure out what he wanted from his life and he needed to do it now before he fell any harder for her. Because once he fell in love his options would change. They had to. And he wasn't ready for that to happen.

Why had he thought that he could sleep with Molly and it wouldn't be anything other than physical?

She'd always been the one woman he'd never been able to forget.

JASON DIDN'T SAY much the next morning as he drove his late-model sports car through the Houston traffic. They'd left the ranch early but still hit traffic on US 59 as they'd approached the city.

"The last time I was here was for college," Molly said, trying to engage him in conversation to take his mind off the tests.

"You never did say why you left."

She nibbled on her bottom lip, looking out the window at the other commuters creeping along the highway. What could she say? "It was a relationship. That was the real reason. Annabelle's messiness wasn't actually that hard to live with."

"What happened?"

She rubbed the back of her neck. She didn't like to talk about it. Who did? Breakups were messy, painful and embarrassing. "I fell hard for this guy. He seemed to fall for me, and then…life happened. He got called back home because his mom was sick and while he was there he fell out of love with me. End of story."

"That doesn't sound like that's all there is to it."

She sighed. "He'd been gone from school for two weeks and we had been texting…and he was sort of being distant. I thought his mom had taken a turn for the worse."

She remembered everything about that time.

"What happened?" Jason asked as he signaled to exit the highway.

"Well, I was worried so I went there to see him. He'd hooked back up with his high school girlfriend. He was going to tell me when he got back to Houston. Didn't want to break up over the phone, blah, blah, blah. I just wanted to die. Not so much because of the emotions, though they hurt, but because I'd been so foolish. I misjudged him."

"His mistake," Jason said. "He missed out on something special."

She had thought so at the time, but now, feeling what she did for Jason, she knew that the college boyfriend had never been right for her. He'd been someone new and different but not the love of her life. "It took a while for me to realize that. I wasn't sure I'd ever be able to trust myself and my judgment with a guy again."

"Who changed that for you?" he asked.

"Do you really want my romantic history?"

"I guess not. I was just… I wondered how you got over it."

She wrapped her arms around her waist and thought about it. "Going home was the best tonic for that heartbreak. Made me realize what was really important. Dad and Rina both let me have some time to figure things out and that was all I needed. I started to realize it was mainly humiliation I was feeling, not really a broken heart. That helped the most. What about you? Ever had a broken heart?"

He glanced away from the road for a moment to look at her. Then he turned his attention back to the traffic. "I don't think so. I've been pretty casual in all my relationships. Didn't want anything to interfere with my commitment to NASA."

"What about now?" she asked. As soon as the words left her mouth, she wished them back. She stared straight ahead and tried to pretend she hadn't just asked him how he felt about her.

"I'm not sure. You're different, Molly."

He pulled up to the security gate at the space center and lowered his window to talk to the guard. Then he started driving again. She had more questions, but now wasn't the time. She was disappointed, she admitted to herself as he parked the car in front of the program manager's office, but she tried to shake it off. She tried to compare what she felt now to what she'd experienced back in college and it was impossible.

There was no way to equate a crush and her first sexual experience with what she felt for Jason.

He looked over at her and she sensed he knew she was thinking about what hadn't been said in the car.

"Want to meet my boss?" he asked.

Not really. But this was what she was competing against for his affections. She should learn as much about the program and the people involved as possible. If he was cleared to return to space, they were the only part of him that would be left here in Texas. And she would be working with them on the training facility.

"Sure."

She slung her purse over her shoulder and walked up the steps, aware that she looked like a country mouse who'd come to the city. But it didn't bother her. She was who she was. Jason put his hand on the small of her back as they entered the air-conditioned building and walked down the long hallway past crew photos and pictures of different missions. She tried not to look at them, but she couldn't help it. She didn't want to see "Ace" in his element because then it would make it real that he belonged at NASA and not on the ranch with her. When she saw a large photo of Jason by himself in his space suit, holding his helmet, she stopped and stared.

She saw the intensity in his eyes and she knew then that she was being silly about a man again. There was no way a woman could compete with something that made him feel that way. It wasn't just his career. It was his calling. Being an astronaut was who he was. He belonged in the space station or exploring a distant planet, not repairing fences on the ranch.

14

AFTER INTRODUCING MOLLY to Dennis Lock, Ace went to Dr. Tomlin's office. She ran the blood tests as soon as he arrived. Then he was put through a battery of other tests, which included simulations of space-enforced gravity, zero gravity and pulling Gs. Ten hours later he was exhausted and felt as if he'd completed an Ironman triathlon and followed it up with a marathon. His body was tired and he ached. He had been running at the ranch, following the diet plan that Dr. Tomlin and Mona had outlined and doing other chores and the extra weight training Molly had interrupted. But he'd hoped for more time and more warning about the tests.

"I'm beat," he said to the doctor when she came back in to take his blood again.

"Good. That was my intention. I want to create a good baseline for you before you train for your next mission."

"Will I be going on another mission?" he asked.

"I don't know yet. But that's the goal," she said. "You can go home now. Be back here at 9:00 a.m. tomorrow for another round of tests and I should have more of the results then."

"Will they be final?"

"We will see," she said. "I still haven't found anything conclusive. The raised calcium levels in your blood were alarming when you got back and I didn't see them improving at the rate I expected after your intensive rehabilitation. But so far we've seen no development of kidney stones."

"Was that a concern?" he asked. "I spent a lot of time on the ARED when I was up there. Way more than the recommended two hours a day."

She put her hand on his arm. The ARED was a treadmill that was used on the ISS and equipped for the astronauts to use in microgravity. "I know. Believe me, no one wants your results to be promising more than me. A lot of your routine over the last year was based on my theories."

He nodded. He knew everyone was anxious to see how he'd improve. "How do I match up with the other candidates?"

"I'll need to see all the test results to get the full picture, but, based on what I've seen today, this is what I can tell you so far. Your improvement at the six-week mark…isn't the same as theirs. In some areas you are way ahead."

"Which ones?" Ace asked. He'd keep doing whatever worked.

"Muscle strength and stamina. But your blood work…that still has a long way to go. It could be due to the extra three months you spent up there."

He wanted to punch something, like maybe the

wall, but—given the state his bones might be in—that didn't seem like a wise choice. "What can I do?"

"Continue with the diet and exercise program you've been following. I've invited Candice O'Malley to meet with you shortly. She is having a different recovery than yours. Maybe you two can share notes."

"Sure," he said, glancing at his watch and noticing he only had ninety minutes until he was supposed to meet Molly at Rocket Fuel. He figured he was going to need a beer after this day. "I thought I'd be done by eight."

"You will be."

"Okay. Where is she?"

"Get dressed and meet me in my office. We can talk there."

Ace got dressed quickly, but didn't want to leave the examining room. He pulled out his phone and sent a text to Molly.

Ace: Might be a few minutes late. <bashful emoji>

Molly: Okay. I'm at Rocket Fuel with Hemi and your other astronaut friends.

Hemi? Damn. He'd forgotten he'd told his friend to meet him there later. He wanted Molly to get to know the astronauts who would be using the training facility on the Bar T. He'd been feeling like he had everything under control earlier. Well, sort of. He'd felt like he was some sort of superman and not...*broken*.

Dr. Tomlin hadn't said it, but he could tell she'd been disappointed with his results.

Ace: Don't believe everything he says. He likes to exaggerate.

Molly: I noticed. You okay?

Ace: Not sure yet. Talk to you soon.

Molly: <kissing emoji>

He rubbed his chest. She'd sent him a kiss. He knew that sleeping with her was making them closer, strengthening the bond between them. But her texting him a kiss made things feel more real somehow. Or maybe it was just an emoji, he reminded himself. He sent her one back and then pocketed his phone. Health first. That was easier to deal with than his emotions.

SOMEHOW HER TABLE had become a gathering point for astronauts while she waited for Jason. Mostly because of Hemi, who seemed to know everyone. More and more people crowded in and around the booth. Hemi ordered wings, insisting that they were so good she had to try them. And she heard more stories about Jason's missions.

Molly was surprised at the number of women in the group and learned that there was an equal number of both sexes on the team.

"Can I sit here?"

Molly glanced up to see a woman with thick blonde hair who could easily have been a model. She was of average height and her bone structure was good, and Molly knew from studying art that she had the golden triangle of proportions.

"Sure. It's mainly astronauts coming and going, though."

The woman laughed. "I am an astronaut. Isabelle Wolsten, but everyone calls me Izzy."

"I guess I don't really get away from the ranch much," Molly said. "Sorry, I didn't realize you were one of the astronauts. I think most of my ideas about the NASA program are from reruns of *I Dream of Jeannie* and, of course, news coverage about the space shuttles."

"NASA has had a low profile in the press for the last few years while they changed direction. Trainees are only accepted every four or five years and the training process takes a year and a half before the selections are made. My class was half men and half women. But we were the first," Izzy said. "What do you do?"

"Cowgirl," Molly said. "I grew up on a ranch about sixty miles from here with Ace."

"You know Ace?" Izzy asked.

"Yeah."

"What was he like as a kid?" Izzy asked, taking a sip of her iced tea. "He's so intense. I can't imagine him as a child."

"I only knew him from the time he was fourteen. He was intense and brooding then. Kept to himself, especially in the beginning."

Izzy raised both eyebrows at her. "Was he cute?"

Molly felt herself blushing again. "Sort of."

Izzy laughed. "I had my suspicions."

"About what?" Jason asked, joining their group.

"You being a cutie way back when," Izzy said, sliding out so that Jason could sit next to Molly. Izzy sat back down, forcing Jason so close to Molly that she felt the tension in his body.

He reached for a wing, his arm grazing her side. "I don't know about that. I didn't spend much time looking in mirrors—I was too busy staring up at the night sky, dreaming of seeing the stars and planets up close."

"Weren't we all," Hemi said.

Molly rested her shoulder against the wall and listened to all of them talk about how they'd come to NASA. She thought about what Izzy had said, that half of her group had been women, and how much things had changed.

They left about thirty minutes after Jason arrived. He was quiet as they drove toward downtown rather than to his quarters on base.

"Where are we going?" she asked.

"A hotel. Is that okay? I've had enough of NASA for today. And I thought it might be nice to do something we don't get to do often. Go someplace and be pampered. Sleep in a king-size bed with you and forget the world exists."

That appealed to her. More than he could know. He hadn't spent all day as she had—realizing they were truly from two different worlds. Even building a training facility on the Bar T Ranch wasn't going to provide them with a ton of common ground. It would be good to avoid all the reminders of their differences, at least for a little while. But she knew there must be something else driving Jason to this decision.

"Okay. That sounds nice," she said, putting her hand on his thigh.

He covered her hand with his, lacing their fingers together until they pulled up in front of one of the big-name hotels in the downtown area. He gave his keys to the valet and checked them into a large luxury suite.

It was a three-room suite, the kind she'd read about in travel magazines and had seen on television shows, but had never been in one herself.

Jason started kissing her as soon as the door to the suite closed behind them. He had her clothes off and her on the bed in record time. He brought her to climax again and again, but held himself back until finally—when she felt as if she wouldn't be able to come again—he entered her, thrusting hard, driving her higher.

She came with him and then collapsed against him. He lifted her up and carried her into the shower, holding her in his arms as the warm water poured over them. Mentally and physically exhausted, she rested her head against his chest.

He held her to him and she realized he hadn't spoken since they'd entered the room.

"What did the doctor say?" she asked when they were both dried off and in bed.

But he didn't answer her. and when she lifted her head and stared down at his face, his eyes were closed.

But she knew he wasn't sleeping.

It must have been bad news for him. Was that why he was clinging to her so closely?

15

WHEN THEY GOT back to the Bar T the next evening, they learned they'd won the bid for the Cronus training facility.

Lynn flew into Houston two days later and joined them at the ranch soon after. Construction needed to start immediately, and Molly was hopeful this would snap Jason out of the funk he'd been in since they'd returned. It seemed like he'd shut himself off from her. He hadn't said what the doctor's prognosis was, but it didn't take a genius to figure out that it hadn't been good.

Lynn was fun and very used to being in charge. She arrived on the ranch with her assistant and spent three days at the location where the facility would be built. Jason was with her every moment, and when they came back for dinner on the first night, Molly was pleased to learn they, NASA and Axiom, wanted to name it the Mick Tanner Cronus Training Facility. She was really touched they'd named it after her dad.

So why wasn't she sleeping now? She was walking that long dark hallway again, but this time there was no Jason out here to join her. She realized that was what she was waiting for. When had she become so cowardly? She should just go and knock on his door…but she was unsure he would want to see her. She had the feeling he was fine with being alone, but she wasn't.

She didn't embark on affairs lightly, and this was the most intense one she'd allowed herself to have in a really long time. She just felt…well, very adult now. Her parents were both gone. She had no close relatives. She was alone in the world except for her extended ranch family. It had taken her a little while to get used to that feeling.

She walked to Jason's room and stood there staring at the door.

The answers to her questions were on the other side. All she had to do was raise her hand and knock. She could do that.

Hell, she *would* do that.

She was a Tanner. They never backed down. Maybe she should get that tattooed on her body to remind herself.

Molly rapped on his door and waited. Heard the bedsprings creak and then the heavy sound of Jason's footsteps before the door opened a crack. He looked through, saw her and opened the door wider. He'd pulled on a pair of jeans and had zipped but not buttoned them. The fatigue written in every line of his face made her heart ache.

"Can I come in?" she asked, but she'd stepped forward as she'd posed the question, and he moved back to allow her in.

He closed the door and leaned back against it. A

small night-light illuminated the room and she thought about how most of the conversations they'd had so far—the heavy ones—had taken place in the near dark.

"What do you want?" he asked. There was no belligerence in his tone at all, just weariness.

"What's going on with you?"

"Nothing."

"Jason, enough of this. Based on your reaction from the moment you came back from the doctor's office in Houston, I can only guess that the medical exam didn't go as you'd hoped.

"So?"

"So. Your life isn't over. You talked me into this Cronus program and I need you to be present and help me with it. I know you've been inspecting the site with Lynn for the last three days, but I'm your partner, too. And I'm out of my depth here."

He rubbed the tattoo on his side. *To boldly go.*

"If this is something you can't do—train others to go on missions when you're grounded—then say so now. There are decisions that have to be made if you've changed your mind about being involved in this."

"I'm not going to change my mind, Molly. I'm a man of my word."

She took a deep breath.

"At this moment you don't seem like the Jason I know. You seem like you're defeated. If you need to take some time, then do it," she said. "Maybe it's not my place to tell you what to do, but I don't know what else to say."

He pushed away from the door and stalked over to her like a predator coming after his prey. She mentally shook herself. She'd come in here and poked at him until he'd reacted. She wasn't sure if she was prepared to handle whatever he dished out.

"I needed to hear that. I am dealing with the fact that there is little I can do to improve my bone density. I'm also a bit freaked out that after spending the last few years training to be the first commander of the Cronus missions, I might not be in that position."

She sat down on his bed and looked up at him. "I get it. I really do. I was completely thrown when Dad died. I figured that my life would take one path and all of a sudden I was faced with something I hadn't anticipated. Sure, I knew Dad would die one day, but I thought... I never imagined it would happen so soon. I never pictured the ranch without him."

"Dammit, Molly, you make me feel like an asshole," he said, sinking down next to the bed, resting his head on the mattress. "I am feeling sorry for myself."

"I know. I did the same thing. The situations are as different as they could be, but our reactions—the heartbreak we feel at not having life go the way we want it—that's the same."

He leaned over, putting his head on her knee and hugged her leg to him. "I'm sorry. I haven't been handling this very well at all."

"It's okay," she said. "I can give you more time to adjust, but I just need to know that you are going to be back here with me soon. I need your guidance when it comes to all this space stuff."

JASON HAD BEEN brooding since Dr. Tomlin had given him her rather vague but still grounding prognosis. He hated it. And he had been acting like a brat. But it was hard to mourn the probable death of your dreams. Maybe he should have stayed in Houston and talked to people like Dennis, who'd made the move from active astronaut to program manager successfully.

But he hadn't been able to because of everything he'd put in motion with the facility. He was stoked that the training center was going ahead. Who wouldn't be? The opportunities that would come from it were numerous. And while he'd been thinking all along about how generous he was, saving the day for Molly, maybe he should have been thinking more about what it meant for him.

She was right. She couldn't do this on her own and he was pretty sure Mick was trying to figure out a way to kick his ass from the beyond.

Her words had been humbling. He knew she'd meant them to demonstrate that she understood where he was coming from.

"It's hard to remember that you are still dealing with your grief. You always seem to have it together," he said.

"Ha. You know me. I'm a big mess and I always have been. But no one is going to put up with that kind of attitude here. Rina would probably make me scrub the floors or something until I straightened up."

He smiled. That sounded a lot like Rina. "I should probably volunteer for a few days of floor scrubbing."

He felt her hand on his head, just rubbing gently. "You can have a rain check on that. We need you to liaise with Axiom."

He laughed, but it sounded hollow even to his own ears. She was trying. Too hard, he realized. She wanted to know what was happening with them. He sensed it. He'd been avoiding anything personal from her.

"I'm sorry. I know it's not enough, but I am sorry."

"It's okay. I think you've lost yourself a little bit. You were always confident you were going to get into NASA. Being an astronaut became your identity... I get that."

She rubbed the light stubble on his jaw and looked down into his eyes. Always, he radiated confidence, but at this moment it was banked.

She imagined if she'd had to sell the ranch she might feel like Jason did now. Ranching was in her soul the same way that being an astronaut was in his.

She shifted on the bed. "Come on, get up," she said.

He slowly got to his feet.

"Now, take a seat."

"What are you doing?"

"Distracting you," she said, as she put her hands on his shoulders and then straddled him. Reaching for the hem of her nightshirt, she pulled it up and over her head and tossed it on the floor. Next, she took his hands in hers and brought them to her breasts. She felt his cock moving under her, lengthening and hardening, and she moaned as he squeezed her breasts.

She rocked back and forth over him as her head fell back. His palms moved in a circular motion over her nipples, making them hard and intensifying the need deep inside her.

This wasn't the patient lover she'd had before, she realized, as he moved his hands to her waist and rolled her beneath him. He pushed his underwear out of the way and drove into her with one quick hard plunge that set off a chain reaction within her.

She called his name as she met his thrusts with equal intensity and they both came hard and fast, clutching at each other. He stayed on top of her for a couple of minutes, keeping his weight on his arms as his breath sawed in and out. Then he rolled to his side and she lay there wrapped around him. Neither of them said a word. But she felt…damn, she felt like everything had changed between them.

She cared for him. She was hesitant to use the L word but it was there in her mind. She squeezed her eyes closed, trying to hide from the truth.

She disentangled his arm from her leg, slid off the bed and put her nightshirt back on. "I know how you feel. And as much as I would miss you, if I had the power to make it so you could go on this mission, I would do it."

HE LOOKED AT HER. Somehow without his intending it, she'd become his best friend. She got him. She understood him in ways he wasn't too sure he wanted anyone to, but she did.

"Mol," he said, "what am I going to do?"

She came closer to the bed and touched him gently. "You'll figure it out."

"How?"

"I have no idea. But I know you will. And I can promise that it's not going to be what you expect, but it will get done, anyway."

"I'm sorry I've shut you out," he admitted.

"Me, too. I was worried you'd treat me like a consolation prize if you couldn't actively participate in the Cronus missions," she said, turning her face away from him.

Damn. He'd worried about that himself. He'd been afraid that he'd make her his whole life because he wouldn't know what else to do. That fear was still there.

What kind of man turned to a woman when he no longer knew who he was?

Jason couldn't answer that. Hell, he kept hoping... but hope wasn't realistic. For the first time in many years he felt as he had when his mom died. He'd spent all those nights praying it was all a nightmare, that he'd wake up hearing her key in the door...

Now he knew that hope was a fool's dream. And he needed to own this new life.

Parts of it weren't bad. Not at all.

This bond with Molly was something that soothed the savage part of his soul. The part he'd always tried to suppress and hide from everyone. Finally, he didn't have to anymore. And that was what he'd been waiting for. Space had given him the accolades and the career he'd always craved, but Molly had given him back a piece of himself that he'd never realized was missing.

"Thank you," he said.

She put her hand on his shoulder. "You don't have to thank me. It is partially selfishness that brought me here. I need you."

She needed him.

He thought of all the men he'd been pretending to be for his entire life and knew that in this moment he had to stand up and do it for real. She needed him and he wanted to be the man who was there for her.

He shifted to the edge of the bed, sat up and put his arm around her, hugging her close to his side. "I think I need you, too."

"Think?"

"When Mom died, I promised myself I'd never depend on anyone again, but I feel different with you."

MOLLY KNEW THAT Jason was a man who'd lost everything, so letting his words affect her as deeply as they did probably wasn't wise. But it was hard not to. He was the man she'd always wanted. She wished she'd known that long ago, but it was something that had only been revealed with time.

"I'm different with you, too," she admitted. "I almost didn't come here tonight. You wouldn't have believed how timid I felt standing in the hallway."

"I can believe it. I've wanted to reach out, but I feel so broken. And I know the kind of man you deserve. The kind of man I thought I was. And now—"

"Stop it," she said. "You are still the man you always were. It's just a change in direction, not a completely different path. You won't be cut off from everything you've known and done before."

He stood up and put his hands on her shoulders and she had the feeling that maybe she was making it too easy for him to be with her, devaluing herself. She wanted him. But she needed to be wanted for herself. Not as an outlet for his mixed feelings about his own future at this moment.

But then he leaned over and kissed her, whispered in her ear how glad he was that she was there with him.

He lifted her in his arms and carried her back to his bed.

"Talking about our feelings is different for us," she said.

He gave her a half smile. "It is, but maybe this is how we will be from now on."

"From now on?" she asked.

"Yeah, you and me. This isn't just a fling, is it?"

She propped herself up on her elbows. She'd come here to get him motivated and make sure he was committed long-term to the facility and in some small way to her. Of course, she wanted whatever was happening between them to last, but something didn't feel right.

"It's not a fling, but I think we should take it day by day, for now. You are going through a big change…"

"Don't you trust me?" he asked, putting his hand on the bed next to her hip and leaning over her.

"Maybe," she admitted. "I think you are confused about what's going on with your career. You haven't even told me the doctor's latest prognosis. Are you out for good? Is there a chance you could be called back to active duty?" she asked.

She had a lot more questions, but having come in here and nudged him out of his melancholy she wasn't ready to stop. She needed to know more before she just said yes to Jason. And it wasn't like she had tons of other offers or men waiting for her. There was just Jason and a part of her acknowledged there would probably only ever be him. She realized he made her feel alive and in love. And she didn't want to take a chance on ruining that feeling by letting herself believe he also loved her when he just needed a distraction from his life.

"Okay," he said, moving over to sit next to her on the bed. He propped a pillow behind his back and leaned against it.

"Okay?"

"Yeah, I'll tell you what the doctor said. The change in bone density, while positive, is small. I mean, if I only make progress at the same rate over the next six weeks…" He trailed off and she realized that before this he'd believed he could easily lick this bone-density problem, but now he wasn't sure.

He'd taken a hit to his confidence.

"Okay, well, I don't know much about your recovery, medically, but I do know that you sound like a man who's given up and that's not the Jason—Ace—McCoy I know," she said.

"You're right. No one knows for sure—even Dennis said he wouldn't decide until the initial three months were up. He was hoping that Doctor Tomlin would find something concrete and she'd be able to give me a green light early. But seeing how little things had improved was a wake-up call," he said. "No matter how hard I work or how well I eat I might not be able to fix this."

"What kind of wake-up call?" she asked.

"The kind that makes a man take stock of his life. If I'm not going to be on the Cronus missions, then I need to make a life for myself here on Earth."

"With me?" she asked.

"That's what I want, but I get that you aren't ready to commit to me until we know for sure."

"That's not it. Life doesn't work like that, does it? We can't predict what's going to happen next. If we could, I'd have been prepared for Dad's death and for you coming back here. And you would have known you were going to have health problems," she said. She was trying to guard her heart. That was why she'd thought they shouldn't commit to each other, but the truth was she already had fallen for him and he wanted her.

"I was scared. Trying to keep myself from getting hurt if you went back to Houston and started to go on long missions again, but the truth is no matter what we do after tonight it will still hurt if you leave."

16

THE NEXT MONTH flew by as the facility on the eastern part of their property went up quickly. They got a lot of local interest, and Rina's brother's construction company was hired to redo the bunkhouses and make most of them into astronaut quarters. Lynn flew back and forth but mostly left overseeing the project to Jason and Molly.

He wasn't himself, but then he was still dealing with the possible loss of his dream and trying to adjust to the idea of a new role in NASA.

Molly wanted to believe the way Jason smiled at her and talked about the facility's future every night before dinner, but she saw past it. He wasn't the kind of man who could spend the rest of his life so close to what he keenly wanted but couldn't have.

But on mornings like this when she was riding next to him checking fences, it was easy to delude herself that they would be together for a long time. That the love growing inside of her was really growing between them.

"Sunrise is always my favorite time of day," she

said, handing him the thermos of coffee that she'd brought in one of her saddlebags.

"Really?" he asked. "I like sunset."

"I knew that," she said. That was when the stars and planets were prominent and Jason's dreams of being up there were stronger.

"Just like I know that you like to get out of the house first thing to beat the heat of the day."

"Well, it is Texas, and it does get hot in July."

"Yeah, it does. What's on the schedule for today?" he asked.

"Nothing. The construction crews are done. Rowdy, Rina's brother, said that once NASA signs off on everything we'll be ready for the interior fitting. Which isn't his thing. So today everyone has the day off."

"Everyone?"

"Well, Jeb has a skeletal crew doing the chores, but then we're going to have a barbecue by the pond. Good food, swimming and celebrating."

"Sounds good," he said. "Is Lynn here?"

"She is, along with a few of the other experts that have been hired," Molly said. "I was pretty excited that Jessie Odell agreed to do the survival training."

Jason smiled over at her. "I forgot you two knew each other. She's one of your oldest friends."

"She is," Molly said. She'd been worried about Jessie for the last year. Her longtime lover, Alexi Volkov, had died in his third attempt on Everest. Jessie had been climbing with him when conditions had turned hazardous and he'd fallen into a ravine. Molly had taken a few days to fly to her friend. Later, Molly's dad had died and Jessie had come back to the ranch for a few weeks to keep her company. When the ranch was approved for the NASA facility, Molly had approached Jessie to see if she was interested in being involved in some way. Her friend had decided that she needed something new in her life, and this was it.

"She is. I'm so glad she got this gig. She hasn't been herself since Alexi's death."

Jason turned to look at her, his hands resting on the saddle horn and a straw cowboy hat on his head. "What about you?"

"What about me? I haven't lost my lover, have I?" she asked.

He shook his head. "But your dad died. How are you feeling now?"

She thought about it. She was so different now from the woman she'd been six months ago when Dad had died or even since the beginning of May when Jason had come back to the Bar T Ranch. She thought she'd evolved. "I think I might be Molly 2.0. A new version of myself."

He threw his head back and laughed. "I guess that makes me Jason 4.0."

"I guess so. Are you happy?" she asked. "Sometimes I think you are, but other times…it feels like you're trying too hard."

"I am trying," he said. "That's all I can do."

"I wish I could make this easier for you. Find a way to fix this."

"You can't. All I can do is continue to work out and hope for the best," he said.

He pushed his hat back and looked over at her. She wasn't sure she liked what she saw in his eyes.

"I keep telling myself I have a very slim chance.

But I doubt that much has changed since the preliminary tests in Houston."

"What if it has?"

He looked at her and shrugged. "I don't know. I just don't know what's going to happen. I feel stronger. It doesn't mean I'll be cleared to go back."

But he still hoped he would be—she could tell. This wasn't a surprise, but she felt hurt and embarrassed anyway that she'd been falling in love with him and he'd been biding his time. She should have known better. She *did* know better, but she couldn't help herself and she definitely couldn't deal with these feelings right now. She clucked to Thunder and loped away from Jason.

But there wasn't enough land even on 760 acres to run away from her emotions or her heartbreak.

JASON WATCHED HER go and knew he had to go after her. Working together to integrate the new facility with the ranch during the last month had been nice. More than nice. He'd seen a life he hadn't thought he'd ever find. One that hadn't been his dream but that he was coming to enjoy and feel more at home in every day.

He hadn't been completely truthful with Molly just now. Each week he sent a sample of his blood to Dr. Tomlin. She was watching his calcium levels and last night he'd gotten an email from her that said she saw some improvement. She'd also shared some new information about Candice's blood work. Candice was scheduled to go back up to the International Space Station in one month's time. She'd do a shorter stint, the shortest that NASA ran, just four weeks on the station, and then she'd be back for another evaluation. He wasn't sure what all this meant for his prospects and he didn't want to worry Molly until he knew for certain.

But whatever happened, he knew he didn't want to lose Molly. So he followed her across the fields. His horsemanship had improved drastically since he'd come back here in May.

He pulled Carl—now his personal horse—to a stop as it struck him that leaving the ranch and Molly wasn't going to be easy. His commitment to her wasn't just something to get him through losing the career he'd always wanted, he realized, now that there was a possibility of him returning to active duty.

But how could he say that to her? Despite everything they'd said to each other, she seemed to think that he was either going to stay on the ranch forever or it was over between them. Didn't she?

He clucked and nudged Carl with his heels to get him moving again and finally caught up with Molly at the pond. She'd dismounted and left her horse—a well-trained horse would stay even if the reins were just left on the ground rather than being tied to something. He did the same with Carl. He found Molly on the path and followed slowly.

She turned when she heard his boot steps getting close and he noticed she'd been crying.

"Molly."

She just shrugged and shook her head. "I want you to stay. I want to be enough for you and not have to compete with NASA. I know it's selfish."

He reached for her, but she stepped back and he dropped his arm awkwardly to his side.

"You are enough for me. Sometimes I think I'm not enough for you," he said, tackling the easiest problem first. "These past months have been…an awakening for me. Never in my life had I imagined I'd find a place to call home that wasn't part of the space program."

She watched him with those wide, weary eyes of hers and he was aware that he had to do and say the right things now. Because he loved her.

He stumbled over the thought in his mind.

He loved Molly. He couldn't say for sure when it had happened. Maybe he'd loved her since the first night he'd come back and she'd dropped all her barriers and let him see the real woman. Or maybe he'd loved her since he'd first seen her dark eyes and chestnut braids.

"I'm glad you feel at home," she said. "You always kept a part of yourself isolated when you lived here before."

"I know. I've been afraid to trust another person. It's easier at NASA because it's all about rank and performance, but this—" he gestured to the two of them "—this is scary because the last time I thought of home like this was before my mom died."

She nodded. "It's different for me. This has always been my home. It's hard for me to imagine being anywhere else. But you've always wanted to leave, even when you were a kid, to get out there in the stars. I can understand it, but it's hard for me to figure out how we could be together if you're still able to go on missions. You'd be gone for such long periods of time."

"It would be hard," he admitted. But it was his life. He loved Molly and he loved space. He didn't think he could choose between them. If his health forced him to be grounded, it would be easier in some ways. The decision would be out of his hands. But something deep inside of him felt that he had improved enough, that the exercises and treatments Dr. Tomlin had prescribed had done their job. And that would leave him in a situation he never thought he'd be facing.

"So what are we going to do?" she asked.

"Just keep on the way we have been for the last month. Nothing has changed. I brought it up…well, it doesn't matter. I made a commitment to you and the facility and I'm going to keep it no matter what the tests show," he said.

"Are you sure?" she asked.

He had this one moment where his conscience battled with him. He loved Molly.

Love.

He couldn't remember the last person he'd loved. His mom, he supposed, but that was so long ago she'd faded into a distant memory and sometimes he couldn't remember her face. But Molly was here before him. Standing there looking very unlike herself with her arms wrapped around her waist.

She needed him. He had a chance to become like the strong, caring men he admired. But he'd have to give up his dream.

Wasn't that what love was?

Sacrifice?

He didn't know for sure, but he made his choice. "I'm positive."

TWINKLE LIGHTS AND tiki torches illuminated the dock area and beach around the pond later that evening. Music, laughter and raised voices filled the air. Molly wandered among the ranch hands, construction crew and astronauts who'd come out for the party. She hadn't seen Jason in the last thirty minutes, but that was okay.

They had spent a lot of time alone today before everyone had arrived. She was worried she'd forced him into a decision he'd come to regret.

"What are you doing over here looking all pouty, sunshine?" Rina asked as she came up to Molly and handed her a plastic margarita glass.

She took a sip of the frozen strawberry goodness. "I think I might have manipulated Jason today to do something he doesn't want to."

"Damn, girl, I wasn't ready for that," Rina said. "I thought you were sad that the facility would be opening soon."

It was the end of the Bar T Ranch she'd always known, but she'd made her peace with that. "Change is inevitable, right?"

"Yes, it is. So what happened with you and Ace?" Rina asked.

The two women moved away from the party area down the path where there was a bench nestled under a willow tree. "Remember when I used to think no one could find me here?"

"I do," Rina said. "It was your spot. Your dad told me how you and your mom used to spend time under this willow."

"We did. I always think of her when I come here. I wonder what she'd say about all this," Molly said.

"She'd be proud of you. You've done what was needed to keep the ranch in the family and you are making it a place for future generations," Rina said.

Molly wondered if that was true or if Rina was just

saying what she thought she needed to hear. The truth was someplace in between, Molly reckoned.

"So…" Rina said, taking another sip. "What did you do?"

Molly finished her margarita and sat down on the bench.

"Jason is feeling better. He thinks…he thinks that going on another mission might not be out of the question for him."

"Was it ever?" Rina asked, coming over to sit down next to her.

"Yes. He has been part of an experiment for bone-density loss. It's called spaceflight osteopenia. When we went to Houston right before we won the bid, the doctor saw him and the news wasn't good. He thought he'd never go back to space. So he started considering a future with me and the ranch…"

"Well, damn."

"Exactly. And today…well, today he tried talking to me about it, but I was all like it's me or the moon." She groaned, embarrassed. "I used to be afraid he would leave. No, I would think, what if Jason goes on his mission and when he comes back he doesn't want this or me anymore?" she said. God, she hadn't realized that was what she'd been feeling, but now that the words were out she felt freer.

Rina hugged her close and rubbed her back. "All I know is that love doesn't come if you force it. If that boy loves you, then he won't be able to go into space unless he knows you'll be here for him when he returns."

"You think so?" Molly asked.

"I do." They sat for a few minutes in silence. "I

guess we should go back to the party," Rina said finally.

"We should."

She followed Rina through the branches of the willow and up the path only to run into Jason coming down.

"I was looking for you," he said. He wore a pair of tight-fitting jeans and a dress shirt, along with a Stetson she'd never seen before. He had two glasses in one hand, a bottle of Maker's Mark in the other.

"I'll leave you two alone," Rina said, walking past him.

"I was hiding out."

"Under the willow?" he asked, draping the arm with the glasses over her shoulder.

Everyone knew her secret spot, she thought, and was reminded again that on the ranch there were no true secrets.

"Yes."

"Good, let's go there now. I want to be alone with you."

He led her back under the willow tree. The music from the party was softer here. He put the glasses down on the bench with the whiskey bottle and drew her into his arms.

She started to speak, but he put his finger over her lips. "No more talking. I want to dance with my woman."

He pulled her close, one arm wrapped around her waist, and took her right hand in his left. The radio was playing Sara Evans's "I Could Not Ask For More."

Jason swayed with her, singing under his breath along with the music. She felt her heart melt and fell even more in love with him. And she knew that she could never be the reason this man didn't go for his dreams. That as much as she needed him here by her side, she needed him to be happy.

She rested her head against his chest and sang along with him. Jason started smiling when she looked up and she caught her breath. It was a real smile, not one of those fake ones he gave everyone most of the time. He swung her out and spun her back into his arms, wrapping his arms around her and singing into her ear.

She felt alive and happy. And suddenly she knew what she was going to have to do. Because she wanted Jason to have the life he'd always wanted. And that life was up in the stars.

17

MOLLY LOOKED AT herself in the mirror a week later and almost didn't recognize herself. She had few opportunities to get dressed up. With the updo, the makeup and the cocktail dress, she looked like a different woman. Not a cowgirl but a woman who belonged in the big city. The special liaison for the Cronus training facility. Molly found she was excited about the new space exploration program and her part in it.

Next week an administrative assistant would arrive at the ranch, and Molly was going to have an office in the new building. She shook her head in disbelief.

It didn't seem like that long ago that she'd been standing on the porch at the Bar T wondering what she was going to do without her dad by her side. She'd found a new life. A life she would never have imagined. The road had been hard, but she was in a good place here.

The facility would be welcoming its first group of trainees next week and this gala was to thank all the people who'd worked so hard to get them to this moment.

She'd made up her mind that if Jason was cleared for flight she'd encourage him to take the Cronus crew position Dennis wanted to offer. He had been with Dr. Tomlin all day doing tests. Molly tried to convince herself she was prepared for whatever happened.

She'd purchased her dress with Izzy's help at the Neiman Marcus at the Galleria. It was sparkly and slim-fitting, hugging her curves, with a halter neck and a skirt that ended a few inches above her knees. She'd even stopped into Victoria's Secret to pick up some nice new lingerie. She'd been practicing walking around the hotel room in her new high heels for the past hour.

Her dad used to bring her to Houston to go back-to-school shopping every year in August. They'd book a hotel near the Galleria and either Rina or Annabelle would go with her. Dad would meet them for lunch and then they'd do more shopping. It had been a little odd to visit the Galleria without him.

Jason and Molly had booked the same suite they'd stayed in last time since the gala celebration was being held in one of the ballrooms in the same hotel. Rina and Jeb had come to Houston for the celebration, as well. They were going to meet the initial group of trainees who would be using the facility.

She took another look at herself in the mirror as she fastened the large diamond-cluster earrings that had been her mother's.

You look too pretty to be my daughter.

She glanced around expecting to see her dad standing behind her. But it was just his voice in her head. The words felt like a hug, as if she'd gotten his approval—not just for her appearance, but for everything she was doing. She closed her eyes, realizing that the pain she'd felt when he'd died was starting to ebb. She still missed him, but she could think of him now without crying and that was a very good thing.

She gave her reflection a wink before grabbing the small beaded handbag that matched her dress and heading down to the ballroom. The hallway leading to the ballroom was lined with large posters of all the astronauts who'd done the work leading up to the Cronus missions. She saw Hemi's and Izzy's posters before stopping in front of her Ace's. It was impossible to think of him as Jason when she stared into his intent blue gaze. The photo was of him in his flight suit, holding his helmet under his arm. And under the image was a quote attributed to him.

I grew up on a ranch in Texas so nothing is daunting to me. I need to be out there going where no one has before and expanding our boundaries the way the first settlers did in the West.

As much as she wanted him by her side, she knew that Ace really was a space cowboy. A man who should be exploring the universe, not tied to the land as she was. It was what he was meant to do and she loved him more for it.

"Hello, gorgeous."

She turned to find him standing behind her in a tux. She almost forgot to breathe he was so handsome. His hair was neatly combed and he smiled when he bent down to kiss her. They'd come so far since he'd walked up to her porch on that warm May evening.

She threw her arms around him and started laughing. He joined her, swinging her in a circle.

JASON HAD AN engagement ring in his pocket from Deutsch & Deutsch Jewelers. They had been in business in Houston for more than eighty years and their motto—Where Life Happens—seemed to suit him and Molly. He'd picked it up earlier in the day, after he'd finished the battery of tests Dr. Tomlin had run.

She'd been excited by the test results for the blood samples he'd been sending her each week via private courier. His calcium levels were normalizing. She hadn't seen the same results with her other patients so he mentioned Hemi's mom's diet and the supplements she'd sent him. Dr. Tomlin had immediately gotten on the phone with Mona and he had a feeling that the meals at the Mick Tanner Cronus Training Facility were going to be heavily influenced by Mona's nutrition plan.

Jason was happy being back on the base. Dennis had called him earlier, but Jason had been at the jewelers. He'd wanted a special ring for Molly and had been examining the one he'd ordered to make sure it was perfect.

He hadn't returned his boss's call because he wanted to ask Molly to marry him before he knew if there was an option to go on more missions.

There were a lot of astronauts who were married, and many balanced work and family. But Jason knew himself. He was either Ace or Jason—he didn't know how to be both.

He'd made a promise to Molly that day by the pond

and he wasn't going to back out of it now. She needed him and he was coming to realize how much he needed her.

She was the first person he'd wanted to call when he'd heard the news from Dr. Tomlin.

And tonight…she was beautiful. She shone more brightly than the stars in the night sky and she was holding on to him and laughing with such joy. He didn't want to dim it. Couldn't be the man who made her eyes lose their sparkle.

"That dress is making it hard for me to remember why we have to be here. I want to scoop you up in my arms and carry you back to our room."

She blushed and then winked at him. "There's no reason why we can't have everything we want tonight, is there?"

"No reason at all," he said. Everything she wanted. This was her night. They'd saved the ranch and were getting ready to open the training facility. They were a couple. They had the rest of their lives together.

"I want to take a picture of you by your poster," she said, fumbling in her handbag for her cell phone.

"Why?"

"So I have both handsome sides of you in one photo," she said.

She knew. He hadn't realized it was obvious to everyone else, or maybe it was just because Molly knew him so well that she saw he was two different men. Not balanced at all.

The ring in his pocket felt heavy and he wanted to propose before he went inside and the lure of his old life took over.

He went over to the poster. Saw the brash, confident astronaut staring back at him. The man in the photo wore a hint of a smile along with tons of self-assurance and swagger. He posed next to his poster and she snapped the picture just as Hemi and his brother Manu came around the corner.

"I told you it wasn't odd to take a picture with myself," Hemi said.

Manu shook his head. "Ace, are you for real? I get this egomaniac wanting to pose with himself, but you aren't as into yourself as he is."

Hemi punched his brother on the arm. "Hey."

"I asked him to do it," Molly said.

Manu glanced over at her and then held his hand out. When Molly took it, Manu brought her hand to his mouth and kissed the back of it. "Apologies, my lady. I'm Manu Barrett, this one's older and more handsome brother."

"She has eyes. She can see that you were a warm-up for me. I'm the perfect one," Hemi said.

Jason just shook his head at them.

"This is Molly Tanner," Jason said, introducing her to Manu.

"Are you part of the astronaut program?" he asked as they all moved into the ballroom.

"Not really. I'm a cowgirl normally. But Ace and I inherited some land that is now housing the new Cronus training facility," she said.

Jason thought it curious that she'd referred to him as Ace. She almost always called him Jason.

"That is really cool. I'd love to hear more about it," Manu said. Hemi left them to go talk to Izzy.

"What do you do?" Molly asked Manu.

"I'm in football. Special teams coach for the professional football league. I used to play for San Diego."

"I think I might get kicked out of Texas for admitting this, but I don't really like the game. I'm more of a basketball fan."

"You were almost perfect," Manu said with a wink.

"Well, she is for me," Jason said, putting his arm around her.

"Not perfect," Molly said, smiling. "I'm as real as they come."

Manu laughed and then moved off to find his brother. Jason took Molly's hand in his and started to lead her away from the crowd.

"Where are we going?"

"I want to be alone with you for a few minutes before everything starts tonight," he said.

She bit her lower lip and then nodded. "I figured we'd talk later, but I can do this now."

Do what? he wondered. He led her to a quiet corner and put his hand in his pocket, feeling around for the ring box. She stood there watching him. And the lights dimmed as the emcee came out on stage.

"Ladies and gentlemen, NASA is proud to welcome you to the Cronus Kickoff Celebration. If you will all find your seats, we have a few announcements to make before we get this party started."

"This is going to have to wait," Molly said.

He was afraid she was right. She turned to walk toward their table and all he could do was follow.

EVERYONE SCURRIED TO their seats and Molly knew what was coming next. Dennis had called her earlier when

he couldn't get in touch with Jason, looking for him.
Since he'd met her and Jason had introduced her as his
girlfriend, Dennis had shared that he had some really
good news from Ace's medical evaluation. That was
all, nothing more specific, but Molly was certain that
tonight Jason was going to learn his place in the Cronus missions had been assured.

"Wait, before anything else happens, I want to ask
you something, Molly," Jason said, tugging on her arm.

She turned toward him, saw the ring box in his hand
and felt her heart sink. She put her hand over his, the
one holding the box.

"Oh, Jason. I don't want to be the reason you can't
have your dream."

"You wouldn't be," he said, but she let go of his
hand and went to their table.

As he followed her, Dennis intercepted him and she
glanced back. Saw the intensity of the conversation. A
selfish part of her wished she'd let him ask that question, but she knew it wouldn't be right.

Rina and Jeb were seated at her table along with
Lynn and her husband, Jimmy. They were a cute couple, funny and lively. They almost distracted her from
the fact that Jason hadn't come back and that the emcee
was back on the stage.

"Ladies and gentlemen, I'm sure all of you are as
excited to be here as we are to welcome you. There
are many phases for the next program that NASA has
been developing. Our eventual goal is to get to Mars,
but before we can do that we have to see how our astronauts tolerate extended missions outside of Earth's
gravity. To that end, NASA is launching the Cronus

missions. I'm pleased to introduce you to Dennis Lock, Deputy Program Manager for Cronus."

Molly sat back in her chair, feigning a calm she was far from feeling. She was ready to smile and stand up when Dennis introduced her, but she wished that Jason was by her side. The fact that he wasn't meant her suspicions were right. He was cleared for flight and would be going on the first mission to establish a way station between Earth and Mars. An eighteen-month mission that would be the next step in fulfilling his dreams.

She wasn't going to worry about where that would leave her.

Really. She wasn't.

Rina reached over, took Molly's hand and squeezed it. "Whatever happens, you'll be okay."

She would be. She was stronger from having loved Jason and spending the last three months with him. He'd given her new excitement for life and he'd helped her save the ranch. There was nothing to worry about.

Except a broken heart.

Everyone applauded as Dennis took the stage. He wore a tuxedo and walked with purpose. He was definitely the right man to be in charge, Molly thought. She knew how much the astronauts respected him. Had heard stories about his own missions that night she'd been at Rocket Fuel waiting for Jason.

That night she had seen him surrounded by his team, in his element. She loved Jason. He cared for her and had said he'd found a home with her. But was that because he'd thought he could never return to his real home?

"Thank you, everyone, for that warm welcome.

This isn't a press conference and there will only be one new announcement tonight. You've all contributed to getting the Cronus missions off the ground. All of your hard work is the reason we are here tonight celebrating.

"I need to thank Lynn and her team at Axiom who put together a top-notch bid for our new training facility and got it built in record time. Where are you, Lynn?"

She stood up and waved as the spotlight found her. Molly felt the tension inside of her grow. She couldn't stay another minute. She leaned over to Rina.

"I have to go. Just smile and wave for us," Molly said, talking loudly to be heard over the announcement.

"Sunshine—"

She just shook her head and got up, walking swiftly through the tables with her head down. She heard Dennis talk about the Bar T Ranch and how the facility had been named after Mick as she got to the doors that led to the hallway.

"It's only fitting that this facility be named after the man who was a surrogate father to our top astronaut trainee. The man who has been focused on leading the Cronus missions since I first met him at training camp. I'm pleased to announce that Ace McCoy will be the commander and leader of our first mission."

There were whoops from Jason's astronaut friends and everyone stood up and applauded. Molly smiled to herself. She was happy for him. She thought she'd have to fake it, but there was no need. She finally understood what it was like to love someone so much that seeing them happy was enough. Jason would go on his missions and have his life and the stars. And she would watch from the ground, loving him, missing him and hoping he would come back to her one day.

She couldn't be the reason he stayed and she was pretty sure that she would be if he asked her to marry him. She'd never had to make such a difficult choice in her life, and only by walking out of the ballroom now would she be able to do it.

18

DENNIS HAD OFFERED him the job before he'd made the announcement on stage and Ace had hesitated but only for a moment. He had thought that staying on the ranch with Molly would be enough, but he realized now that he couldn't say no. If he did he'd regret it for the rest of his life and Molly and he both deserved better. He vowed he'd make things right with Molly after the announcement.

He went out on the stage and waved to the audience. When he looked at their table, he noticed Molly's seat was empty. Rina pointed toward the door, and he saw a flash of Molly's dress as she stepped out. He gave Dennis a quick wave and hopped off the stage to follow her.

He was too far behind to see where she went. He checked their suite and found it empty. For a moment he wondered if she'd headed back to the Bar T, but then he spotted her car keys on the dresser. She was still in the hotel.

He had one more idea and followed his hunch up to the top-floor bar that offered a stunning view of the

Houston skyline. He found Molly sitting at one of the tables that overlooked the city. But she wasn't looking at the skyline. She stared at the stars above.

"Mind if I join you?" he asked, coming over to her table.

She turned to look at him, a sad smile on her face. "Not at all."

"Why did you leave?"

"I thought I was ready for it. Dennis called for you earlier today and said that he had good news for you about your medical review. I put the rest together for myself when you tried to propose to me before he could name you as the first commander."

"That's not why I chose that moment to propose—"

"It was. Let's not lie to each other, okay?" she said. "I would have said yes and you would have… What would you have done? I know some of the other astronauts are married, but I think it's always been different for you."

The honesty in her tone hurt him a little. She expected him to walk away from her easily, but he wasn't too sure he could do that. Nothing was easy about this. He wanted the missions and Molly.

"It used to be," he said. "But mainly because I hadn't taken the time to meet anyone who made me…better. You expanded my horizons. Most of my life I've been playing at being an adult, Molly. Trying damned hard to make sure I wasn't the kind of man my 'sperm donor' dad was. The kind of guy who'd walk away from his pregnant girlfriend and never look back."

"You were never going to be that kind of man. You're not made that way," she said.

He appreciated her faith in him. She always had believed in him, especially when he'd doubted himself.

"Regardless, with you I don't have to fake it. You make me the kind of man I've always wanted to be. I love you."

"I love you, too. That's why I want you to go back into space and do these things you've always dreamed of."

"You love me?"

"Yes. I can't imagine a future without you in it."

"Can you imagine a future where your husband leads the first Cronus mission and then comes home, retires and trains others to go on further missions?" he asked.

It was what he wanted. If he could have everything, it would be Molly and NASA and Cronus.

"Are you sure about this?" she asked.

"Molly, nothing can compete with you. If you say no, then I'll tell Dennis to find another commander for that first eighteen-month mission."

She put her hand in his. "I'd never say no. I want all of that for you, for us. I want to be the cowgirl you come back to."

Jason's heart started beating so loudly he was sure the other patrons in the bar could hear it. He got down on one knee and pulled the ring from his pocket.

"Molly Tanner, will you marry me?"

She leaned forward, putting her forehead on his. "Yes, I will."

He put the ring on her finger and got to his feet, lifting her into his arms and kissing her like he would never let her go. And now he knew he'd never have to.

* * * * *

Read on for a sneak preview of
PUSHING THE LIMITS, the next book in
Katherine Garbera's out-of-this-world
SPACE COWBOYS miniseries,
in stores January 2017!

JESSIE ODELL STOOD in the corner of a beautifully decorated room in a converted barn on the Bar T Ranch,
watching the grand-opening party rage on. She'd had
enough of talking about her adventures and the famous
people she'd met. That part of her life had ended when
Alexi had slipped into the ravine on Everest. She'd
pushed on, the thin air and her own drive compelling
her forward, but she'd known once she got back to base
camp the grief would hit her... It never had. She'd become icy inside and out and she'd known that her old
life of making adventure films for television was over.
She was tired of having every moment of her life played
out for the cameras. She was ready for some privacy.

This job at the new Cronus training center was a
godsend.

"Don't like parties much?" a man asked, coming
up on her left.

"Not really," she admitted. He was hard to see in the
shadows. Just the silhouette of a man in a dress uniform.
She could tell he had a strong jaw and dark hair, though.
And he was taller than she was, which was saying some-

thing as she was five feet ten inches and wearing three-inch heels. Her mother had told her to never apologize or cower because of her height, and she never had.

"Me, either," he said. "I'm Thor, by the way."

"Jessie. So I'm guessing Thor isn't your given name. You don't look Nordic."

He laughed and it made her smile. His laugh was full of joy, not rusty, like the way she'd felt inside since Alexi's death.

"Yeah. I guess I should have introduced myself as Hemi. Hemi Barrett. I'm part of the astronaut training crew," he said, stepping from the shadows and holding out his hand.

"You sound American, but that name is Maori, right?"

"Yeah. On my mom's side. She and my pops met in Hawaii and I was raised in LA."

His dark brown beard was close cropped and accentuated the fullness of his lips. Suddenly she realized she'd been staring at his mouth for much longer than was acceptable. She felt a spark of instant attraction she'd never experienced before. For her, sexual desire usually stemmed from knowing a man, and grew out of their friendship.

But this was different. He was different, and this was definitely lust.

His eyes were also dark. Orbs of melted chocolate, decadent and sinful. His skin was tanned and there were laugh lines around his eyes, as well as a one-inch scar on his forehead above his left eye. There was a mark around his left eye as well, she saw—a birthmark. The Maori people called those with these marks *nga kanohi ora o ratou ma kua wehe atu*, which meant "the living faces of those who have gone on before us."

Many believed that the wearer had been marked by the gods for greatness.

Her parents' research had kept them in New Zealand for two years when she'd been in her early teens, and Jessie had learned a lot about the Maori.

He arched one eyebrow at her and she realized she must be staring at him, but didn't care. She had grown up in nature. Her first instincts were always driven by the laws of the wild. In the animal kingdom and in life, she'd found she never regretted standing her ground.

His lips curled in a half smile and he took a step closer. She put her hand on his arm. She felt the strength in him under the fabric of his suit jacket and flexed her fingers on it. All the men she'd known were lean from surviving in the wilderness. Not like him—he was muscled, powerful.

His handshake was firm, but not intimidating the way some men's were.

"Jessie Odell." He said her name with a hint of awe. He must have seen her show or read one of her books.

"Yes."

"Wow. I used to watch your parents' show when I was a kid," he said.

Well, thank God for that. She'd rather talk about her childhood than her last ascent on Everest. Jessie was a part of so many people's childhoods because of those shows her parents, marine biologists and deep-sea botanists, had made. They had followed in the spirit of Jacques Cousteau and had brought her along on their yacht as they filmed their adventures.

"I bet you hear that a lot," he said.

"Some. Other people want to hear what it was like to survive in the Arctic."

"That's cool," he said with a wink. "But I've been to space."

She laughed, and it surprised her. She hadn't expected to. But he was right. She was hiding because she didn't want to talk about herself in a room full of men and women who'd done something extraordinary, as well.

"What's it like?" she asked.

"Well, you can't hide out like this," he said. "Buy me a drink and we can exchange stories. I want to hear about the time you were in the shark cage off Africa."

"It's an open bar," she pointed out.

"Then you have nothing to lose," he said.

"Okay, let's go."

They maneuvered through the crowd and she saw her friend Molly Tanner. Molly was dancing with her fiancé, Ace McCoy.

"Ace has it all," Hemi said.

"Does he?"

"Yeah. He's been named as commander of the first long-term Cronus mission. Molly has agreed to be his wife. He's got this training facility up and running."

"Do you want that?" she asked.

He shrugged. "That's not really a first-date kind of question."

"This is a first date?" But she felt a little embarrassed that she'd asked too intimate a question. Usually when she met people they were both on their way to do something daring, where the risks were considerable and there was a high degree of probability that not everyone would make it back alive.

"I'm hoping," he said with a wink.

That put her at ease a little. He had charm—she'd

give him that. With his looks and body he probably didn't have to work too hard to get women to fall for him. "We'll see. I still don't know what kind of story you're offering in exchange for hearing about ten-year-old me and a great white."

"The time I did a space walk and became untethered…"

"Obviously you made it back," she said.

"Obviously. But it was pretty dicey for a while. What's your poison?" he asked as they got to the bar.

"I'll have what you're having."

"Ah, I don't drink," he said. "I have to stay in top condition. How do you think I'm doing?"

She skimmed her gaze down his body. His shoulders were muscled, broad and strong, tapering down to a lean waist and long legs. She arched one eyebrow. "You look good, but it could be the cut of your clothes."

He shook his head. "Play your cards right and I might let you see me out of them."

She rolled her eyes at him. It was an over-the-top comment and he knew it. He ordered two cranberry juices mixed with sparkling water and then led the way to a high bar table a bit farther away from the crowd in the center of the room.

When they got to the table, Hemi handed her one of the glasses. Their fingers brushed and a zing went up her arm, leaving goose bumps in its wake. She tipped her head to the side to study him.

"To new friends and great adventures." He took a swallow and emptied half his glass.

"New adventures," she repeated, lifting her glass and taking a sip.

"Why are you at this party?" he asked. "Wait, are you one of the new trainees?"

"No. I prefer to keep my feet on this planet. There are still so many areas I haven't explored," she said, but she knew it was a pat line, no longer true. She'd lost the spirit for adventure. But this man, tonight, had awakened her sense of fun and excitement. She wasn't too sure it would last, but fun sounded like a nice change of pace.

"Then what are you doing here?" he asked.

"I'm the survival training instructor. I'm here to make sure all of you spacemen and -women know how to survive in any condition."

"Oh, I guess we'll be seeing a lot more of each other, then." He grinned, and her pulse sped up as she imagined how much more of him she'd like to see...

*Look for PUSHING THE LIMITS,
coming January 2017, to read the rest
of Hemi and Jessie's story!*

COMING NEXT MONTH FROM

ⓗ HARLEQUIN®
Blaze®

Available September 20, 2016

#911 HIS TO PROTECT
Uniformly Hot! • by Karen Rock

Lt. Commander Mark Sampson hasn't been the same since he left one of his rescue swimmers in a stormy sea. Too bad the beautiful stranger he just spent the night with is the man's sister...and a Red Cross nurse assigned to his next mission!

#912 HER HALLOWEEN TREAT
Men at Work • by Tiffany Reisz

If the best way to get over someone is to get under someone else, handyman Chris Steffensen is definitely repairing Joey Silvia's broken heart. But is Joey's high school friend a guy she could really fall for?

#913 THE MIGHTY QUINNS: TRISTAN
The Mighty Quinns • by Kate Hoffmann

Lawyer Tristan Quinn poses as a writer to start a charm campaign against the residents of a writer's colony who are staunchly opposed to selling. But his fiercest—and sexiest—opponent, Lily Harrison, isn't buying it. So he'll have to up his offensive from charm...to seduction.

#914 A DANGEROUSLY SEXY SECRET
The Dangerous Bachelors Club • by Stefanie London

Wren Livingston must hide her identity from her to-die-for neighbor, Rhys Glover, while he investigates the crime she's committed. But hiding her attraction to him proves impossible after one particularly intimate night...

HBCNM0916

"I'm going to go up and see what he's doing." Joey saw a
large green Ford pickup parked behind the house with the
words *Lost Lake Painting and Contracting* on the side in
black-and-gold letters.

"I'll stay on the line," Kira said. "If you think he's
going to murder you, say, um, 'I'm on the phone with my
best friend, Kira. She's a cop.' And if he's sexy and you
want to bang him, just say, 'Nice weather we're having,
isn't it?'"

"It's the Pacific Northwest. In October. It's forty-eight
degrees out and raining."

"Just say it!"

"Now, go check him out. Try not to get murdered."

Joey crept up the stairs and found they no longer
squeaked like they used to. Someone had replaced the old
stairs with beautiful reclaimed pine from the looks of it.

"Hello?"

"I'm in the master," the male voice answered.

Joey walked down the hallway to a partly open door.

There on a step stool stood a man with dirty-blond hair cut neat and a close-trimmed nearly blond beard. He was concentrating on the wiring above his head. He wore jeans, perfectly fitted, and a red-and-navy flannel shirt, sleeves rolled up to his elbows.

"Hey, Joey," he said. "Good to see you again. How's Hawaii been treating you?"

He turned his head her way and grinned at her. She knew that grin.

Oh, my God, it was Chris.

Chris Steffensen. Dillon's high school best friend. That Chris she wouldn't have trusted to screw in a lightbulb, and now he was wiring up a ceiling fan? And seemed to be doing a very good job of it.

"Did you...did you fix up this whole house?" she asked, rudely ignoring his question.

"Oh, yeah. I'm doing some work for Dillon and Oscar these days. You like what we did with the place?"

He grinned again, a boyish eager grin. She couldn't see anything else in the world because that bright white toothy smile took over his face and her entire field of vision. He was taller than she remembered. Taller and broader. Those shoulders of his...well, there was only one thing to say about that.

Joey hoped Kira was still listening.

"Nice weather we're having, isn't it?"

Don't miss HER HALLOWEEN TREAT by Tiffany Reisz, available October 2016 wherever Harlequin® Blaze® books and ebooks are sold.

www.Harlequin.com

Reading Has Its Rewards

Earn **FREE BOOKS!**

Register at **Harlequin My Rewards** and submit your Harlequin purchases from wherever you shop to earn points for free books and other exclusive rewards.

Plus submit your purchases from now till May 30th for a chance to win a $500 Visa Card*.

Visit **HarlequinMyRewards.com** today

Earn **FREE** REWARDS Join Today! HarlequinMyRewards.com

MYR16R1

HARLEQUIN®

A Romance FOR EVERY MOOD™

Stay up-to-date on all your
romance-reading news with the
Harlequin Shopping Guide,
featuring bestselling authors, exciting new
miniseries, books to watch and more!

The newest issue will be delivered right to you
with our compliments! There are 4 each year.

Signing up is easy.

EMAIL

ShoppingGuide@Harlequin.ca

WRITE TO US

HARLEQUIN BOOKS
Attention: Customer Service Department
P.O. Box 9057, Buffalo, NY 14269-9057

OR PHONE

1-800-873-8635 in the United States
1-888-343-9777 in Canada

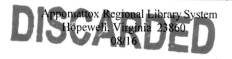